"I can't believe is pulling out

"Shhh!" Raven glared at her sister and turned back to the television.

"There you have it, folks. In the political upset of the year, a candidate that polls favored by a three-to-one margin has withdrawn his name from the race for the senate with only six weeks left until the primary. Matthew Strong's decision is final, based on personal reasons, which he apparently has no intention of revealing."

With a sigh, Raven switched off the set. Tense silence reigned in the room and she knew her family was struggling not to ask *the* question. Finally, she could take the tension no more and she shot to her feet. "Okay, yes. It's Matthew."

"Your Matthew?" Her father looked at her over half-glasses.

"Yes." She rubbed her throbbing temple with the balls of her fingers in an attempt to ease the pressure. *My Matthew.* Regret for what might have been all those years ago shot through her. She hadn't allowed herself second guesses. No regretting her decision. So why was her heart suddenly about to pound out of her chest?

Books by Tracey V. Bateman

Love Inspired Suspense

*Reasonable Doubt #4
*Suspicion of Guilt #6
*Betrayal of Trust #8

*The Mahoney Sisters

TRACEY V. BATEMAN

lives in Missouri with her husband and their four children. She writes full-time and is active in various roles in her home church. She has won several awards for her writing, and credits God's grace and a limited number of entries for each win. To relax, she enjoys long talks with her husband, reading, music and hanging out with her kids, who can finally enjoy movies she likes. Tracey loves to encourage everyone to dream big. She believes she is living proof that, with God, nothing is impossible.

Tracey V. Bateman

Betrayal
of Trust

Steeple
Hill ®

Published by Steeple Hill Books™

STEEPLE HILL BOOKS

Steeple
Hill®

ISBN 0-373-44224-6

BETRAYAL OF TRUST

Copyright © 2005 by Tracey Bateman

www.SteepleHill.com

Printed in U.S.A.

Behold, what manner of love the Father has
bestowed upon us, that we should
be called the sons of God.
—*1 John* 3:1

Lovingly dedicated to the memory of my dad, Rodney Devine Sr., who passed away several years ago. He always made me feel safe.

Also to the memory of my father-in-law, George Bateman. I had no doubt that he loved me. There is no one like this special man, except perhaps his wonderful son, my husband.

And to my Abba. Father to the fatherless. God in Heaven. Thank You for adopting me into Your family.

Prologue

Matthew Strong pulled his car into the wooded rest area of the forest reserve and watched a man approach wearing army surplus and tennis shoes. Even from ten feet away, Matthew noticed the grime on his hands. His stringy, greasy hair was held in place by a filthy bandana folded to look like an Indian headband. He sauntered, his shoulders moving with a cocky assurance that grated on Matthew's nerves.

Fighting to contain his disgust, Matthew pressed the automatic unlock and the man slid onto the tan leather seat, his stench powerful enough to bring down a bear.

"This is the one and only time I'm going to do this," Matthew said without a greeting. "So if you're planning any kind of ongoing blackmail, you can forget it now."

Ray Marx gave him a two-fingered salute as he tugged on the handle and slammed the door, closing them inside. His lips curled in a smug sneer that left Matthew fighting for control. "Really nice of you to meet me. Got a cigarette?"

Without bothering to respond to the ridiculous question, Matthew pulled an envelope from the pocket on the driver's side door.

Silently, and for effect, he fingered the bulging manila envelope. Ray's eyes followed every trail of his thumb in anticipation. His foot tapped in a nervous beat to no discernible rhythm. Anticipation of what? Drugs? More than likely. But Matthew couldn't worry about that right now. Not when his child's safety was at stake.

"I see eight years in prison didn't do you much good. How long did it take to find a fix? An hour?"

"What are you, my parole officer?" Ray reached for the envelope, but Matthew snatched it back.

"We're going to get a few things settled first."

"I said all I got to say to you on the phone. Give me the money or I go to the papers. They might be interested in hearing about the daughter you stole from me."

Anger burned in Matthew. He slid his hand inside his Armani jacket and produced a document. "Are you forgetting this?"

Ray's eyes narrowed. "What is it?"

"You signed away your rights to her. Remember? The adoption is legal. No court in the country would revoke that. It's all a matter of public record. I have nothing to hide."

Matthew watched the drug dealer carefully. There was no emotion in his eyes other than greed and perhaps a trace of anger to see the truth in black and white.

He shrugged. "I was forced into signing."

"We both know that's a lie."

"A lie? I'm truly hurt. And here I've been dreaming of the day I get out of prison so I can be a real daddy to my little daughter. Think of all the things I could teach her."

Matthew clenched his fists to keep from dragging the clown out of his car and pummeling him to within an inch of his life. But he knew that would do no one any good. Least of all Jamie, his eight-year-old daughter. "But that's what this little envelope is all about, isn't it? Your promise to go away and pretend you've never heard of my sister, let alone fathered her child."

"And I thought it was just about a friend helping a friend."

"Sure you did."

"Well, if you're not going to play nice, give me my money and I'll leave you alone."

"That's what I intend to ensure before I hand over a dime." Matthew narrowed his gaze and stared until Ray squirmed under the intensity. "Do not go near my sister. Is that clear?"

"Yeah, yeah. I got all I needed out of that one, anyway. Give me the cash and let me go."

Matthew handed over the package.

With his filthy, grease-embedded hands, Ray deliberately opened the envelope and riffled through the cash. Pretending to count. Slow, sly, like the coyote he was. A predator. The dregs of society. Not worth the dirt under Casey's dainty feet.

Dear, God. Why couldn't I have protected her from having a relationship with a man like this?

Ray finished counting and looked up. "Just one more time to double-check." And he started the process again.

Matthew balled his fists. In two seconds he was going to…

Dan Ackerman, Matthew's semi-retired attorney, shifted forward from the back seat. He slapped down hard on the leather headrest above Ray's head. The seat shook.

Ray jumped, his Adam's apple moving up and down in his throat, his eyes shifting in an obvious attempt to suppress a rush of fear.

Grim satisfaction flowed through Matthew.

Dan fixed Ray with a glare that allowed for no more stalling. "You know it's all there. Get out of here and stay out of Matthew's sight, if you know what's good for you."

Obviously trying to maintain his dignity, Ray slid the money envelope into his dirty army jacket and made smug eye contact with Matthew. "Thanks for the new start. I'll be seeing you."

Matthew sprang with the agility of a mountain lion. He grabbed Ray by the scruff of his neck and slammed him against the window.

"If you come near my sister again, I'll make you wish you'd never heard the name *Strong*. Do you understand me?"

He felt Dan's hands on his shoulders. "Matt, don't give him any ammunition."

Slowly, Matthew allowed reason to return. The blind rage lifted and he unclenched his fists, releasing handfuls of wrinkled jacket.

"Unlock the safety so he can get out," Dan said.

Matthew flipped the switch. The coyote slunk against the door, then got brave as the handle gave way beneath his hand.

"Give my girl a hug for me." He smirked. "Tell her Daddy loves her."

Fury exploded in Matthew and he went for Ray again, but the coward anticipated the move and jumped out just before Matthew could grab hold. He fled into the woods without looking back.

Dan grabbed Matthew before he could go after the man who had ruined his sister's life nine years earlier. She had finally come to her senses that night, just before Ray nearly beat her to death. That was also the same night the police had picked him up on probation violation and new drug charges. But the arrest was made too late to save Casey. The thought of this man back in their lives filled Matthew with rage.

"I'll kill him!" The image of his battered twenty-year-old sister haunted him. Her bouts with sickness. The revelation that she was carrying her abuser's child and the knowledge that she wouldn't, couldn't, have an abortion.

Casey had delivered the baby, but remained a shell of the girl she'd once been. The last beating had damaged her brain and left her with severely diminished mental capacity, unable to raise a child. Despite the efforts of all the doctors who did their best to fix her, she would never be the same.

Jamie, named after Matthew's father, was born healthy and wonderful. Matthew had raised her as his own daughter. Now this monster was back, threatening to take his so-called story to the press. Threatening to accuse the Strong family of using their substantial influence to gain his arrest in order to get rid of him—get him out of Casey's life. Of course, he'd be willing to stay quiet for the right price.

Matthew waited while Dan left the back seat and moved to the front. He was fairly confident Ray would not speak a word about the Strong family. He only hoped he had bluffed the man enough to stay away. But he couldn't be certain. And that uncertainty was the prompt for his next course of action.

Matthew's jaw ached from his clenched teeth.

With a glance at his gold watch, Matthew tried to stop his heart from racing. He'd taken care of one problem for today. Now it was time to move on to the next item on his agenda: end his career. He'd been groomed for public office since the day he was born. Thirty-seven years in the making. Destroyed in five minutes.

"What time is the press conference?" He kept his tone even, though it took a conscious effort to keep a quiver from his voice. He would give a brief statement and take no questions. The subject of his withdrawal wasn't up for discussion. After this first and only pay-off, he would take away Ray's only ammunition against the Strong family: Jamie.

"Matt, you sure you want to do this?"

Matthew nodded. He felt raw. Spent. Ready to get it over with. "There's no choice. If I'm not in the public eye, Ray will have no ammunition against me. No one's going to care enough about my private life to try to hurt my sister or my daughter. It has to be this way."

Chapter One

Raven Mahoney's jaw dropped as the sickening thud of truth slammed her with the force of a major-league line drive to the gut. While she'd been playing the dutiful maid of honor and helping with wedding preliminaries for her sister, Denni, she'd just missed out on reporting the press conference of the year. As far as Raven was concerned, that smacked of injustice.

From the TV screen in Denni's living room, cameras flashed at dizzying intervals. Raven could almost feel the claustrophobia she experienced every time she stood among the crowd of reporters, fighting for the chance to ask a question.

And she almost always got her chance to ask the tough ones, but not so tough the speaker wouldn't respond. She knew her success was a nice combination of her looks (especially if the speaker was a guy) and her instincts about how to ask the right questions so they sounded less intimidating. At thirty-five, she'd gained a lot of savvy in her field and she was ready to move one more step up the ladder of success.

Only, the teenybopper on the screen in front of her

was getting the story, she, Raven should be getting. Something akin to a growl rose in Raven's throat, and her predatory nature kicked in.

Enjoy the cameras while you can, little girl, because as soon as I get home, you are going down.

Raven closed her eyes and imagined herself at that press conference. Where she wanted to be. Despite the jumble of cameras and elbows jabbing into her head, she itched to be in the thick of things. To prove, once again, her value to the station. Ten years on the job had to count for something, didn't it?

Her chest tightened, and pressure began to build. But this time, the claustrophobia struck in the living room of her soon-to-be-wed sister's Victorian home. Being in the bosom of her loving family suddenly felt more like standing in a trash compactor as the walls inched closer and closer together until finally they squished her, a sensation that had grown familiar over the past few years, ever since her mother's death, when she'd learned the truth about who Raven Mahoney really was.

In retrospect, it all made sense, but the revelation only served to make her feel more like an outsider in the midst of this family—and all these years later, Mac still hadn't set the record straight. Nor had Raven. Mac had no idea she knew. And as angry as she was with him for keeping the truth from her, she didn't have the heart to confront him.

"I can't believe Matthew Strong is pulling out of the race." Keri, Raven's younger sister, married barely a year herself to her childhood sweetheart, flopped onto the overstuffed green couch next to Raven. "I was going to vote for that guy."

"Shhh!" Raven glared at her sister and pressed the volume-up button on the remote.

"Sheesh, so-o-rry."

"What's going on?" Denni, the middle sister, entered the room, her eyes on the TV.

"Shh, or you'll get your head yanked off." Keri's exaggerated whisper resonated through the room.

"I'll talk if I want. It's my house. Besides, I'm the bride and everyone must cater to my whims. So there." Denni stuck her tongue out at Raven.

Raven rolled her eyes at the childish gesture, but couldn't resist a smile before shifting her focus back to the TV.

Her claws extended at the sight of the so-called reporter staring out from the screen: Kellie Cruise, an upstart and a spoiled-rotten brat—way too under-qualified and inexperienced to be covering a press conference. Especially one of this magnitude. But nepotism at its finest continued to be at work for the daughter of the station manager. And Raven knew if she didn't act fast, the just-out-of-college kid was going to get Bruce King's job when he retired. The job that Raven wanted. Deserved.

"What's going on?" Mac Mahoney's booming hint of an Irish brogue filled the room.

"Shh!" The three girls spoke in unison.

"Hey, now. Is that any way to speak to your father?" He scowled, but quieted, as his attention turned to the blond-haired, blue-eyed reporter who was wrapping up the breaking-news coverage.

"We've been told that Mr. Strong will not be answering any questions on the subject of his withdrawal. Now or ever. His decision is final and is based on personal reasons which he apparently has no intention of revealing."

The camera shifted back to the studio where the white-haired, almost-retired anchor stared out at the TV audience.

"There you have it, folks. In the political upset of the year, a candidate whom analysts and polls favored by a three-to-one margin has withdrawn his name from the race for Senate with only six weeks left until the primary." The older gentleman heaved a sigh. "To reiterate…with no warning to his supporters and no explanation, Matthew Strong has pulled out of the race for the Missouri Senate."

If he'd said, "And may God help us all," Bruce couldn't have been more obviously biased. It was only too apparent that he had had high hopes for Matthew's election to Senate. No matter how much she might agree, Raven couldn't help but be a bit irritated with his transparency. Part of good reporting was remaining detached, keeping your opinion carefully masked behind the facts and nothing else. Perhaps it was simply that after so many years behind that desk, Bruce didn't feel he had anything to hide—namely his opinion.

With a sigh, Raven switched off the set as regular programming resumed. Tense silence reigned in the room and she knew her family was struggling not to ask *the* question. Finally, she could take the tension no more and she shot to her feet. "Okay, yes. It's Matthew."

"*Your* Matthew?" Mac looked at her over half glasses.

"Yes." She rubbed her throbbing temple with the balls of her fingers in an attempt to ease the pressure. *My Matthew.* Regret for what might have been all those years ago shot through her. She hadn't allowed herself second guesses. No regretting her decision. So why was her heart suddenly about to pound out of her chest?

She could still see Matthew's expression of bewilderment as she'd placed the diamond engagement ring into his palm and curled his fingers around the token. She'd walked away. Transferred to a different school. And that was the last time she'd spoken to him.

Keri's voice brought her back to the present. "Wow. I wonder what his folks think of him leaving the race. He was a surefire win for his party. Especially with his father dying last year. I don't think Missouri is ready to live without a Strong representing us in Congress. What was Matthew thinking?"

All eyes turned to Raven as though she should know the answer to the question. "How should I know? I haven't seen or spoken with the guy since college."

Raven fingered the cell phone hooked to her waistband. She itched to phone Ken at the station and get the scoop. The press had to know more than they were reporting. No one pulled out of a race without giving some sort of an explanation—even a bogus one. Was there a gag order? She was tempted to make the call, but doing so now would betray her impatience to have this wedding over with so she could get on with her life. She'd been here two days as it was—long enough. Too long, actually, from the looks of things.

Matthew! Couldn't you have waited a few more days to do this idiotic thing?

Fingering a loose thread on the arm of the couch, Raven considered the new development. What could have happened to make Matt give away the chance eventually to run for president? That was his dream, his goal, not only to follow in his old man's footsteps, but actually to exceed his accomplishments. His family had groomed him for the White House. He'd had no other ambition except for marrying her. And other than the monkey wrench of a broken engagement, his plan was failsafe—undergrad, law school, interning under an incumbent senator, eventually running for senator himself and serving his constituents until it was time to run for president. Raven was supposed to have helped him decide when the time came. They would have been in their late forties, probably, by the time he was seasoned enough and ready to win the White House. And she'd had no doubt that with or without her he would someday be the president of the United States.

Now what would he do? Return to his law practice? Given his fame, that might be difficult.

She clenched her fist to keep from snatching the phone from its holder. If she could just get back to work, she could figure all this out.

"No way, Rave. You are *not* wimping out on my wedding, so you can just forget it. I don't care how big the story is. My wedding is more important. And you're not ruining it by leaving me one bridesmaid short."

Jerked from her thoughts by Denni's firm statement, Raven mustered up her most indignant and wrongfully accused expression. "I can't believe you think I would consider leaving before the wedding."

Denni rolled her eyes. "*Pul-ease.* I recognize that 'get me out of here before I suffocate' look. You're trying to think of a way to weasel out of my wedding so you can go back to Kansas City today—and don't bother to deny it."

Heat crept to Raven's cheeks. "All right. You have me. It crossed my mind for a second. But that's all—and not really seriously."

Denni's responding scowl increased Raven's shame. She hated feeling guilty and it seemed like she always felt guilty around her family. They expected too much. More than she could give. She knew she was a terrible sister, a terrible daughter. Her gaze focused past her sister to Mac Mahoney. The gruff, but tender retired Irish cop who had raised her, loved her, taught her never to settle for second best at anything in her life.

He looked up from studying the TV listings and his eyes crinkled with his smile.

Raven fought to hold back tears of melancholy.

She might feel like a terrible daughter, but then, she wasn't *really* his daughter at all, was she?

The door to the sleek black Lincoln closed behind Matt amid the flashing of cameras and a myriad of questions thrown at him from determined reporters hoping he'd actually answer one. But they didn't understand. His public image didn't matter anymore. Only one thing did at this point: keeping Jamie out of the line of fire perpetuated by a biological father with ulterior motives. No telling how far that man might go to extort money from the family. He'd never get custody of Jamie, but he could drag them all through the mud. And that wasn't something Matt was willing to chance. He'd sacrificed everything to ensure it.

"That's that," he said into the airspace between the front and back seats. The driver gave him a quick glance in the rearview mirror and then returned his attention to the road as he realized Matt wasn't speaking to him.

Exhausted, Matt slouched back against the leather seat and pulled at his silk tie, loosening its stranglehold around his neck. A tangle of frustration, disappointment, anger, all rolled into a lead ball in his stomach, nauseating him.

Leaning his head back against the seat, he closed his burning eyes. He refused tears. Refused to regret his decision. It was the only choice he could have made. The right choice.

Still, he had to wonder how a life that had been so

carefully planned could have ended up so off-course. By now he should have been married with two or three kids of his own, should be six weeks away from accepting his party's nomination for Senate, and only a few months from the next step in his destiny: Capitol Hill, the springboard to the Oval Office.

Backtracking in his mind, he could see that everything started going sour the day Raven Mahoney returned to school after attending her mother's funeral. He should have gone with her to her hometown of Briarwood, Missouri, in the first place, but she'd insisted it was something she had to do on her own. Her stubbornness was never more evident than when she was trying to prove she didn't need anyone to lean on. He scowled.

He'd watched her career evolve through the years as a reporter and weekend anchor for Channel 23. She grew more beautiful by the day, it seemed. His throat tightened with longing. No matter how many women he'd dated over the years, he couldn't get Raven out of his mind. No one measured up, and any relationship he entered into ended within months.

He clenched his fists, still able to feel the prick of the diamond against the soft flesh of his palm when she'd broken their engagement. Maybe it would have been easier to accept…easier to move on…if only she'd told him why.

For the first time in his life, he'd been helpless to achieve his goal. Never had he felt such pain as when he watched Raven walk away from him. He'd hoped she'd glance back, knowing if she did, he could go after her and bring her back to him. But she squared her shoulders, kept her head erect, and never so much as slowed her steps as she walked out of sight.

When he'd spotted her on the local news, it had been

all he could do to refrain from picking up the phone. But she'd made it pretty clear he wasn't the man for her. So he left her alone, but found himself watching her left hand for signs she might be engaged or married. So far, so good.

"Do you want to go in through the main gate, Mr. Strong? Or should I keep going?"

Matthew glanced at his driver, and then out the window. The gate in front of his family home was thick with reporters. "No. Drive on by. We'll circle for a while. Maybe they'll get tired and go away. If not, I'll stay at a hotel."

They drove the streets of Kansas City until dark, stopping only once at a drive-through. The greasy burger and fries sat heavily in Matthew's stomach as he tried to pray for wisdom. Peace. How long would it take for all of this to blow over and for the media to lose interest? Not soon enough for his comfort. In the meantime, how would he keep his sister and Jamie away from public scrutiny?

Chapter Two

Raven closed the back driver's-side door of her red SUV and searched the wad of keys in her hand for the one to the ignition. She glanced at her glowing digital watch with grim satisfaction. Ten minutes after midnight. At this time of night, traffic would be practically nonexistent. She'd be home in four hours.

"I still think you should wait until morning."

Forcing a smile, she turned to Mac. "I'm wide awake. And this way I'll miss daytime traffic."

Mac sighed and shrugged. "I don't suppose I can force you to do as I say anymore. But be careful and call me as soon as you get to your house—no matter the time. I won't sleep until you're home safe and sound anyway. Lock your doors and don't stop for anyone. Not even flashing red lights. Never know if some sicko bought a strobe light just to fool pretty girls."

"I promise," Raven said around a sudden lump in her throat. It felt nice to have someone concerned about her.

As if sensing her mood, Mac opened his arms. She hesitated only a second before surrendering to his familiar embrace.

"I love you, Raven, my sweet girl. You will meet us at the cabin for the fall barbecue, right?"

"I'll try, Dad. Just depends on how busy I am at work."

"Well, you've got three months to think about it. And make plans."

Raven pulled out of his arms and opened the driver's-side door. She rolled down the window as Mac stepped up for a final goodbye.

"I don't mean to push you, honey. I just miss my girl, that's all. It's like pulling teeth to get you home for a visit."

"I know. I'm sorry. But I'm a busy career woman. When you're married to your job, it takes a lot of TLC to keep the relationship alive." She forced a grin in an attempt to lighten the situation.

Mac looked at her with sad eyes. Another sigh escaped his lips. He leaned in and pressed a kiss to her forehead through the open window. "I just can't help but think there's more to it than just your work."

"Like what?" Raven asked, shrugging with a nonchalance she hoped he interpreted as her way of saying he was being silly to even think there was a problem.

"I don't know, honey. You tell me."

Raven kissed his cheek and then fired up the SUV. "You're just being paranoid, Dad. Nothing's wrong except that that ten-year-old, Kellie Cruise, is about to sashay in and get my job if I can't talk Matt into an exclusive interview."

A scowl marred his features, but his eyes gentled with acceptance. Raven knew he was letting her go without more argument, advice or admonishment. And she appreciated the gesture. He patted her cheek, then walked around to the sidewalk where he stood with his hands inside his pockets.

A blue economy car whizzed by just as she started to pull away from the curb. She slammed on her brakes to avoid getting sideswiped. "Nice driving, buddy!" she hollered after the retreating car.

"Great way to start the trip," she grumbled.

As she drove away, Raven glanced in the rearview mirror. The streetlight illuminated Mac's position. He stared after her, his shoulders slumped. A twinge of dismay stung her heart and she gripped the steering wheel until her fingers ached. They would eventually have to talk, but not today. First she had to deal with Matt. Seeing his face plastered across the screen and hearing his strong, deep voice make his announcement had filled her with a sense of what might have been between them. And along with nostalgia, the pain of Mom's funeral had crested once more on a tide of buried memories.

How different might her life have been if that drunk driver hadn't plowed into Mom's car, killing her instantly? For one thing, Raven wouldn't have discovered the truth about her paternity. Life would have continued as it was projected to go. Marriage to Matthew. Two-point-five kids. Ignorance would have been bliss. Knowledge had darkened the bright light of hope for the future—a future with Matthew. Everything had changed.

Releasing a sigh, she pressed the accelerator with her toe and the SUV picked up speed, heading north on US 63.

Her eyelids grew heavy an hour later listening to Frank Sinatra's silky-smooth crooning, and she stopped at a twenty-four-hour quick stop along the highway to grab a cup of coffee. She grimaced. The black brew smelled as if it had probably been sitting there since the afternoon before. The clerk gave her a guilty look and pronounced it "no charge."

A blast of sultry summer air lifted strands of Raven's sleek black hair off her neck as she exited the convenience store. A motor revved to her left and she turned in time to see a familiar blue car drive away from the parking lot. Familiar from where?

Visions of the back of that car haunted her, keeping her mind busy while she drove the rest of the way to Kansas City. She pulled into her drive and dialed her dad—per his express instructions, no matter what time she arrived—to let him know she'd made it safely to her door.

Her mind went back to the car that had sped by as she was about to pull away from Denni's curb. So that's where she remembered a blue car from. Both small, blue and square. She grinned and shook her head. That was a weird coincidence. Nothing more. Probably wasn't even the same car. Some reporter she was.

"Hi, Dad," she said when he picked up. "Just letting you know I'm home safely, so you can go to bed now and try to sleep."

"Praise the Lord." She could hear the note of relief in his voice. But there was a weariness that she'd noticed lately that concerned her.

"Dad, you feeling okay? When was the last time you checked your blood pressure?"

"I'm just fine, young lady. Don't start sounding like Ruthie."

Raven bristled. The last person she sounded like was Dad's Southern belle of a fiancée. The mention of the woman's name conjured the flamboyant red hair piled atop her head like Flo from the eighties sitcom, *Alice*. The too-cheerful-to-be-real demeanor. The knowledge that Mac could be in love with this type of woman after loving Raven's mother, a classic beauty with more creativity and style in her little toe than Ruth had in her whole body was just too irritating.

"Well, I'll let you go, Dad. Get some rest, okay?"

"You too, hon."

Raven disconnected the call. By the time she'd unloaded her bag, gone inside and showered, dawn was just beginning to glisten over the enormous oak tree in her backyard.

She sat on her deck, wearing a white terry-cloth robe and sipping a mug of strong, black coffee. By 6:00 a.m., she could restrain herself no longer. She snatched up her phone and dialed Ken, her camera guy and the one person she knew would be straight with her. His grumbled, sleepy "Hello" didn't faze her. He'd interrupted her sleep plenty of times.

"Ken, what's going on with the Matthew Strong story?"

"Raven?"

"Who else?" Impatience edged her voice, but after two days of no inside info after finding out about Matt, she'd had all the delays she was going to take. "Matthew Strong?"

For the next few seconds all she heard was the rustling of sheets and the hiss of a lighter as presumably, the grizzled, old-before-his-time, forty-five-year-old sat up in bed and lit a cigarette.

"Those things will kill you, Ken. You need to quit smoking."

"Mind your own business."

"Fine. They're your lungs."

"You got that right."

Raven shifted in her seat, stifling a yawn. "Tell me about Matt."

"Matt, is it?"

Despite the fact that Ken couldn't see her, Raven felt

a blush creep up to her cheeks. "We had a thing once a long time ago."

"What kind of thing?" he asked in his I-smell-a-story tone of voice.

"The kind that's none of your business."

"Touché, but is it perhaps the kind of 'thing' we might be able to use to get access to the almost-senator?"

An uneasy twist affected Raven's stomach and suddenly the coffee didn't sit well. "Just meet me at Corner Coffee, will you? We need to talk and map out a strategy."

"All right, girl. But let me tell you, I'm not wasting my time on personal ethics. If you got an inside to this guy, you better use it or I might take the sweet Miss Kellie up on her tempting offer."

"You're old enough to be her dad."

"Yeah, well. Ain't that the kicker? I'm *not* her dad and she seems to go for my natural maturity. And she likes the way our names go together. Thinks it's downright cute. Kellie and Ken. It does have a nice ring to it, don't you think?"

Raven gave a snort. "Don't flatter yourself, pops. She wants to break up the wonder twins, and that's all there is to her sudden attraction."

It was common knowledge around the station, and had been for the past several years, that Ken and Raven were an unstoppable team. Thanks to Raven's instincts for where the great story was, they rarely failed to bring it home, and thanks to Ken's hot ability with a camera, they ended up with unbelievably good shots of whomever they were after. The dream team.

Raven's ire rose at the very thought that Kellie might be making a play for Ken. And even more so that Ken was exploiting it to bait her into using her past with Matt as a means to an end.

Never mind that she planned to do that anyway, she didn't need someone reading her so easily. It just made her feel more rotten than she already did.

"Stop threatening me. You know Kellie would get on your nerves in three and a half seconds. You'd be miserable. Meet me in forty-five minutes."

Without waiting for a reply, she hung up. A second later the phone rang. A grin split Raven's lips. She snatched up the receiver. "You just have to have the last word, don't you, cowboy?"

"I'm sorry?"

Raven nearly swallowed her tongue at the unfamiliar voice. "Who's this?"

"Um, Sonny."

"Well, Sonny, I think you dialed the wrong number."

"I don't think so. Raven Mahoney?"

"All right, buster. I don't know how you got this number, but I don't take calls from strange men."

"Wait! Don't hang up. If you're Raven Mahoney, then you're going to want to talk to me."

Matthew jolted awake and fought to understand why he could barely breathe.

"Are you awake, Dad?"

A smile lifted the corners of Matthew's lips and he opened his eyes to find Jamie sprawled across his chest, her dark hair sticking up in about twenty different directions.

"I am now, you little twerp!" Grabbing the little girl he wrestled her across the bed and tickled her just enough to be funny. Too long and it was just mean. Matthew wouldn't do that. But they both enjoyed a short wrestling/tickle game.

"Hey, Dad?"

"Yeah?"

"I saw you on TV yesterday."

"You did?" Irritation nipped at Matt. "How come you were watching it?" And more importantly, why didn't his mother keep Jamie away from the set? She knew he wouldn't want his daughter watching.

"The news interrupted cartoons."

"I see."

She stretched out on her side next to him, her ear cupped in the palm of her head as she rested on her elbow. Her eyes dulled with a rare solemnity as she stared at him with concern.

"How come you changed your mind about being senator?"

A lump gouged Matthew's throat. "I just decided it was best."

"Why?"

He caressed his daughter's hair. "Some things are not up for discussion, Jamie. When you're older, I'll explain."

The little girl scowled, looking an awful lot like Ray. Way too much. Matthew's pulse quickened. As if by instinct, Matthew reached forward and grabbed her into a fierce hug.

"Dad!" The muffled voice held a squeak of mild panic. "You're squishing me."

Reluctantly, Matt released her. "Jamie, I want you to listen to me. This is very important. Are you paying attention?"

Wide brown eyes stared back at him, as Jamie nodded.

"You have to be careful. Play close to the house and don't go near the gate. Understand?"

"Why?"

"Because I said so."

She frowned, her freckled nose wrinkling in confusion. "But why do you say so? I always play by the gate."

"Can you just trust me on this one?"

She hesitated, but gave another nod.

"Don't talk to anyone you don't know really well. Even if you see me talking to the same person. Clear?"

"Come on, Dad. What's all the drama about?"

Matthew smiled at his daughter. "There are some things I'm not ready to talk about." *Like the fact that your natural dad is out of prison and extorting money from me. And if I didn't step down from the race, he could have used my position to exploit you.* If Jamie were a few years older, he could have told her those things, but not at eight years old. For now, she needed to concentrate on playing soccer and watching the Cardinals and having a great summer vacation. "Now, are you clear on the new rules?"

She shrugged. "I guess so. Can we go to breakfast now? Grams said we're having blueberry pancakes."

Matthew's favorite. He had a feeling he'd be getting a lot of his favorite dishes over the next few days. Mom's way of consoling him. It was a wonder he didn't weigh a ton.

"Go tell Grams I'll be down in a few minutes."

"Yes, sir."

Matthew took a quick shower then headed down the hall toward the stairs. He paused at Casey's door, tapped lightly, then opened it just far enough to see in. His little sister slept peacefully, her long lashes fanning baby-doll cheeks. She was still so innocent. His heart ached for what might have been. What sort of life might she have had if Ray had never come to work at the mansion as a gardener? A user and an abuser, he'd sweet-talked his way into Casey's life. Her family hadn't discovered the relationship until it was too late—Casey left home, moved in with Ray and lost her trust fund down the black hole of drug abuse. Ray's addiction.

Guilt squeezed Matt's heart. And he thought the same self-condemning words that had repeated themselves over and over during the past eight and a half years.

If only he had never hired the man who had wooed his sister then stolen her innocence.

Chapter Three

Raven mulled over her strange telephone conversation as she wove in and out of five lanes of traffic. She was already twenty minutes late to meet Ken. And Ken didn't like being kept waiting.

Well, he'd just have to get over it. She wasn't going to tell him the caller had been her long-lost half brother. A fresh jolt knocked into her gut at the thought. She actually had a brother?

Sonny Thatcher. Son of Josiah Thatcher...her father. A twinge of guilt pinched at her as immediately her mind conjured the image of Mac. She didn't want to hurt the man who had loved her as his own and raised her with the same loving care as he had her two younger sisters. But how odd to discover her biological father had lived in Kansas City. All these years, they'd shared the same city of residence.

Her conversation with Sonny had been brief. She'd listened to just enough to convince her he might be telling the truth about their familial connection, set up a meeting time and place, then sat on her overstuffed couch and allowed her heartbeat to slow to a steady rhythm for the next ten minutes. She wasn't positive that she even wanted to know these men. But she couldn't shake off her curiosity and had set up the meeting despite her conflicting emotions.

A horn blared behind her as she whipped her SUV into the last lane of traffic just in time to avoid missing her exit. That's all she needed, further delays.

And why wasn't Ken answering his cell phone anyway? Essentially, it was his own fault he didn't know she'd be late. She'd tried to call him four times.

She pulled into the parking lot ten minutes later and breezed into the coffee shop. Ken sat at their table.

"I don't want to hear it," she said putting up her palm. "I have a good reason for being late."

He shrugged. "I just got here, myself."

"Ken! What if I'd been here waiting for thirty minutes?"

He shrugged again. "So, what's your good reason for being late?"

"Forget it. Let's just order coffee and get started."

"I've been thinking about it." He drew on his cigarette, then released the smoke into the aisle where a leggy blonde in a red business suit walked by and glared. Ken gave her a once-over and pointed to the Smoking Section sign.

"I wish you'd stop offending people with those things. Especially when I'm with you. What if they recognize me?"

"You're flattering yourself again."

Raven's cheeks warmed. "What have you been thinking we can do?"

"Most logical? Call him up and remind him why he ever had a 'thing' with you in the first place."

"Hey, don't imply it was less than it was. We had a real relationship. No kissing on the first date, down on one knee, heirloom engagement ring, the whole works. And yes, waiting until marriage for anything more than kissing."

Surprise registered on his face. "So he's the honorable type. That'll help."

Raven scowled. "I don't know if I want to use my past relationship with Matt just to get a story. It cheapens it in a way." The only real relationship she'd ever had. It was a bittersweet memory, but one she cherished all the same.

"If you don't get the story someone else will. Are you willing to let it be Kellie?" He leaned forward. "I'll let you in on a secret a little birdie told me."

"What?"

"Kellie's mother is a club friend of Matthew Strong's mother. Seems they meet once a week for lunch. So you see, Kellie has an inside track to this guy too."

Raven's competitive nature took charge. Ken was right. Matthew couldn't hide forever. Eventually someone was going to track him down and get a story out of him. No way was she going to let that person be Kellie. She stifled a growl. Why did everything have to come to that girl handed on a silver platter? Well, she couldn't have Matthew!

She snatched up her cell phone.

"What are you doing?"

"Calling Matt, what do you think?"

Triumph shone in his green eyes. "You know the number by heart?"

"If it hasn't changed since we were dating. You know I never forget anything. As far as I know he's still living in a wing at his parents' mansion. Since his dad died, he's sort of the man of the family."

Ken rolled his eyes. "Families are a chain around

your neck. You have to cut them loose or you'll never have any peace."

Raven hated when he talked like that. Her head and her heart were constantly in a struggle about family and she didn't like hearing it so blatantly from a bohemian with no morals and no ethics. If Ken weren't such a great cameraman...

She dialed Matt's number while Ken looked on. It rang four times then a child answered. "Hello? Who is this?"

"I'm not allowed to say," the child replied. "Who's this?"

"Is—is this the Strong residence?"

A long pause on the other end.

"Hello? Are you still there?"

"Yes," came the whispered reply.

"Is this the home of Matthew Strong?"

"I'm not allowed to say."

"Who are you talking to, Jamie?"

As if caught playing phone pranks, Raven quickly disconnected.

"What?" Ken stared at her, his eyes asking the obvious question.

"A kid answered. I think I must have gotten the wrong number."

"Maybe it was Matthew's kid."

Raven scowled. "And no one knew about a wife and child? Come on."

"Yeah, that's true. So what now?"

Raven took a sip of the too-sweet, chocolate-flavored coffee and pinched a bite from her muffin.

"Matthew was always a creature of habit. He probably still works out at Randy's Gym on Harrison."

"Mr. Senator at that dive? I don't see it."

"Trust me." Digging into her purse, she tossed some bills on the table, then stood.

"Where are you going?"

"I think it's time to get back into shape. See you later."

With a grin, she exited Corner Coffee and headed to her car. First stop—the sports shop two blocks away. She'd need exercise clothes and gym shoes if she were going to pull this one off.

Now, please God, let Matthew still work out at the gym.

The memory of that phone call this morning irked Matthew. Jamie knew better than to answer the phone. Only the girl's insistence that the caller had been a woman stopped Matthew from calling the phone company and changing their number.

He couldn't explain to Jamie. And that made things hard. The kid was growing more independent by the day. Answering the phone was taboo. She knew that. If one of her friends called, she could talk. But she could not answer on her own. Why had the little girl picked now to start testing the limits?

Dusk was settling as he pulled into the parking lot. His muscles twitched, anticipating the welcome punishment. He knew he could trust Randy not to let anyone know he was coming in to work out. The salty characters at his gym were serious body builders who didn't care if he was a senatorial candidate or a factory worker named Ed. As long as he didn't hog the free weights, they were cool. Never once had he had to deal with the press before, during or after a workout. And right now he needed to sweat. To push his body to its limits and clear his head.

He kicked the treadmill up a couple of more notches

and increased his running speed. His heart responded with the appropriate rise in beats per minute.

The newest CD from his favorite worship band blasted in his ears through headphones, upbeat music lifting his spirits and setting his mind on things above. Soon he became lost in the rhythm of the music and his own body's rhythm as he pounded out mile after mile on the soft surface.

> You're with me on the mountaintop
> When my world comes full stop.
> With me in the darkest times,
> With me when the sun shines bright.
> I know Your hand is guiding me
> In trusting You I find release.

Matthew swallowed down the lump in his throat. Trust had been difficult. He couldn't see where the rest of his life could possibly go. It would be nearly impossible to practice law again any time soon. Too many people knew him. Politics were out of the question—at least until Jamie was grown, and by then, it would most likely be too late.

He supposed he could move to a quiet little town in a different state and start a bookstore or a café or something.

> I know Your hand is guiding me.
> In trusting You, I find release.

I want to trust You, Lord. But I can't see what You possibly have planned for me.

He might have continued the prayer, but movement caught his attention through the mirror in front of the treadmill. A woman entered the workout room. Every eye in the place followed her as she glided to a cross-training machine. Matthew's throat went dry. She looked so much like…

Just then she looked around and spotted him. Her eyes went wide with surprise. Matthew nearly stumbled. To avoid falling flat on his face, he peeled his eyes away from Raven and turned his attention back to the treadmill for just a second to slow to a walk and then a stop. He grabbed a towel and swiped at the sweat streaming from his face, neck and arms as he walked toward her. Not exactly the impression he wanted to make on Raven Mahoney after fifteen years.

Her lips curved into a gorgeous smile that did more aerobically for his heart than the last four miles on the treadmill.

"Matthew," she said breathlessly. "You still work out here?"

Ignoring the twinge of suspicion niggling through his mind, Matthew took her proffered hand, wishing he didn't reek of sweat so that he could pull her to him and bury his face in the silky strands of her hair.

"You know me. This is the only place I can get a decent workout. Luckily the press hasn't gotten wind of it yet."

Her expression clouded.

"I didn't mean you." He smiled.

Relief crossed her features and she smiled back, flashing teeth that were just a little more perfect than he remembered.

"So what have you been up to?" he asked.

"Oh, I just got back from my sister's wedding in Rolla."

"Which one?"

Raven smiled. "Denni. Keri married her childhood sweetheart a year ago."

"So you're the only unmarried Mahoney girl left?"

She shrugged and her nostrils flared a little the way they did when she was trying to pretend she wasn't irritated. "I guess so."

"You didn't have to be." Matthew could have kicked himself. Now why had he gone there? Her expression hardened.

"I'm sorry. That was uncalled for."

"Don't worry about it, Matt. You want to show me how this thing works?" She indicated the cross trainer machine. Clearly the subject was closed.

"How about if I take you to dinner instead?"

"What about my workout?"

He leaned in. "Between you and me, I think you can afford to skip it."

Pink crawled to her cheeks, charming Matt. So the self-assured reporter still had trouble taking compliments.

"What do you say?" he pressed.

She narrowed her gaze and studied him as if trying to gauge his motives. "You know I'm a reporter. What if all this was a ruse just to get a story from you? Maybe I *want* you to ask me to dinner?"

The challenge was more than Matt could resist. He winked. "Then let's just say I played right into your hands." He knew he'd have to be on guard. Still, after all they'd shared he couldn't believe she'd callously milk a story from him with no thought to his privacy.

Still, she hedged. "It's just dinner, Raven. No strings attached." *Unless you want them to be.*

Her expression softened and she nodded. "All right. I've heard these machines are real torture anyway. Dinner with you has got to be preferable."

The teasing glint in her eyes shot through his heart, igniting feelings that had eluded him since he'd watched her walk away. She still had him. Hook, line and sinker, his heart belonged to this woman. All she had to do was say the word and he'd bring out that velvet box containing her engagement ring and pick up right where they'd left off.

Maybe he had a future after all. And maybe that future was wrapped up in Raven Mahoney.

Chapter Four

Raven couldn't believe her luck. She stared across the table as Matt gave the waiter his order and handed back the menu. How was it possible that he'd grown even more handsome during the past fifteen years? A few lines etched the skin next to his eyes and around his mouth, but these served only to give him a mature, distinguished appearance. A few silver strands of hair near his temple added to the effect and Raven found herself wanting to giggle like a nerdy high school girl who had landed a date with the captain of the football team.

One disturbing question probed her mind. How could she have ever led herself to believe she was over Matthew Strong?

He glanced up. A slow grin spread across his face. "I caught you."

Raven quickly averted her gaze to her own menu, feigning nonchalance. "Caught me what?"

"Staring."

"Oh, please." Raven smiled despite her embarrassment. "Still full of yourself, I see."

"What some people see as egotism, others—Mom, for instance—consider confidence."

"Confidence, huh?" Raven tried to control her breathing. Keep it even and light. Not give away her out-of-control feelings. But one look into Matt's eyes and she knew she was fooling no one. Least of all, Matt. The one person who could read her like a copy of the *Washington Post*.

She didn't resist when he reached across the table and took her hand, lacing her fingers with his, forming a steeple. "Why, Rave?"

"W-why what?" She swallowed hard, kicking herself for not preparing for this inevitability. Of course Matthew would grab her heart again. She just hadn't realized he would do it in five seconds flat. That had to be a world record.

"Why did you walk away?"

"I just—had to, Matthew. It's nothing I can put my finger on, really. I just knew it wasn't right between you and me."

"It was right." His thumb traced the sensitive skin between her thumb and forefinger, making it hard for Raven to concentrate. "We were right together."

"I—I don't think so. Life was too complicated. I wasn't ready to commit."

"Doesn't it seem strange to you that we're both still single? Neither of us moved on."

Raven snatched her fingers away and hid her hands in her lap. "What makes you think I haven't moved on?"

Disappointment washed Matthew's features as the intimate moment between them passed. "No ring."

"Maybe I don't believe in conventional tokens of commitment."

He gave a short laugh. "Diamonds are a girl's best friend. Even unconventional girls."

Raven had to smile. Then she grew serious once more. "Just because I haven't tied myself down to a man doesn't mean I haven't moved on, Matt. It just means I'm not interested in a relationship. What I have moved on with is furthering my career."

"I see."

And Raven could tell by the smug relief on his face that he did indeed see. And not what she was claiming, either. He saw into the very truth of the matter. A truth that had taken her by surprise—the fact that he still had her heart. But she wasn't ready to deal with that issue herself, let alone admit it to Matt, of all people.

She fixed him with a dubious rise of her brow. "Oh, please. Don't make this about you."

He held up his hand in truce fashion. "Far be it from me to be so egotistical." But his eyes glinted with amusement.

Raven rolled her eyes. He exuded ego.

"What about you? Why haven't you moved on?" Desperate to get the focus off of her own life and motives, Raven took a chance on the question, knowing he would more than likely open up all the raw wounds between them. This news story had better be worth all the pain.

He studied her, his blue eyes squinting with intensity, as though probing her mind. She squared her shoulders, meeting his gaze evenly, hoping against hope that she had met her objective and accomplished an expression of passive interest.

"Why haven't I moved on?" He leaned back in his seat as he repeated her question. "I guess I never found the right girl. No one measures up to Raven Mahoney. Didn't you know that?"

He was mocking her. Raven knew it and she felt the blush creep to her cheeks in hot trails.

He smiled. "Actually, I've just been too busy. First, with law school. And I have to thank you for all my good grades, by the way—if you hadn't dumped me, I'd have been much too distracted to pass the bar."

"You're welcome," Raven said dryly.

He gave her an appreciative smile for taking the joke as it was intended. "After law school I worked for three years in the offices of Tyler, Hillman and Long."

"Very prestigious. I'm duly impressed."

"As I intended you to be. Thank you."

"You're most welcome." Raven's heart nearly soared at the banter. They had settled into the easy back-and-forth just as though time hadn't moved forward fifteen years without them.

"Then I went to work as an intern in Senator Grady's office. Eighty-hour work weeks don't make for a romantic atmosphere. I barely had time to sleep and spend time with my d—"

An arrow of sharp instinct lodged into Raven's senses. She raised her brow? "Your what? Dominoes? Diary? Dear old aunt?" She grinned.

With an indulgent smile at her attempt at humor, he gave her another studied look, then almost in defeat, sighed. "My daughter." He reached into his jacket and pulled out a billfold. He handed her a photograph. An adorable little girl with brown hair and marked freckles grinned back at her, revealing two missing front teeth. "That's a couple of years old. Her teeth have grown in."

Matt's pride in the girl was obvious.

Questions tripped over each other in Raven's mind until she wanted to give them expression, but she sat up a little straighter and forced herself to hold back. A professional never overwhelmed the interviewee. *Tread carefully, Raven. Don't scare him off.*

"She's cute." She smiled. "Doesn't look a thing like you, though."

"She's adopted."

"Wow, Matt. That's amazing."

"You don't sound amazed." A frown creased his brow.

"I'm just wondering why a single man with a busy and promising career would feel the need to adopt. It's not like you even have a wife to give the child a mother. Why not just find a woman, get married and have a little princess of your own?"

He raised an eyebrow, one corner of his lips tipping in a mocking smile. "Are you applying for the job? Because if you play your cards right—"

"All right!" Raven reached for her water glass with a trembling hand. "You're going to have to stop bringing up our past as though we're still a couple, Matthew. It's....ridiculous."

"Then you're going to have to stop behaving like a reporter. I don't like being interrogated—especially where my family is concerned."

"I *am* a reporter. Remember?"

"Funny, and I thought you were an old friend."

The waiter appeared with their food, effectively cutting off Raven's reply. For the moment. Matthew turned an expectant gaze back to her. "Do you want to ask the blessing or should I?"

Alarm shot through Raven. Matthew frowned, obviously confused by her hesitation. 'Everything okay?"

"Uh—yeah," she said. "You pray."

He did so, then picked up the conversation where they'd left off. "Well?" he asked. "Are you here as an old friend or as a reporter?"

"I didn't realize it was taboo for 'old friends' to ask about family, Matthew. Or is your personal life only off limits to *some* old friends?" It had taken her the five minutes the waiter was beside their table to come up with the proper response, and she couldn't help but silently bless the server for coming to her rescue. Her words nailed him with their intended effect.

"Forgive me," he said. "I tend to live with a bit of an edge lately. Suspicion is my middle name."

"Listen, I understand. I'm not one to discuss my personal life much either. I just thought..." She gathered a deep breath just before hammering in the nail. "I just thought you wanted us to be friends again."

Matthew couldn't put his finger on exactly why he didn't trust Raven. Perhaps because she was a reporter, perhaps because she'd suddenly shown up out of nowhere. Perhaps because she had broken his heart and left a gaping wound to remind him not to trust her.

Friends. She was offering friendship when he wanted so much more. He wanted her love, her adoration, her devotion. He wanted her heart and body—in a pure and holy union before God.

Friendship wouldn't do. He'd rather never see Raven again than be forced into a lesser relationship.

On the other hand, perhaps some time on a friendship basis with her would give her a chance to realize she still loved him. And Matthew knew she still cared. He could read it in her eyes, had felt it in the rapid pulse at the base of her wrist. Perhaps he could finally get an answer—once and for all—as to the reason she had walked away from their love.

"Friends, huh? You're right. All of my friends know about my daughter. So why should you be any different?"

"Well, look. If you don't want to tell me, you don't

have to. We haven't seen each other in a very long time. You might not want to become reacquainted."

There it was again. That feeling she was playing him. Would she be so callous as to use his feelings for her just to bring home a story?

"I want to tell you about Jamie."

"Jamie, huh? Named after your dad." She smiled. "That means you've had her since she was a baby."

"How do you figure that?"

"You named her. I can't see you adopting an older child and changing her name."

Matthew grinned. "Always thinking deductively, aren't you?"

A shrug lifted slender shoulders. "Comes with the job."

"All right. Yes. I took her home from the hospital and she's been my daughter since the day she was born."

"What of her birth parents?"

The question was to be expected. Still Matthew hesitated.

"Not something you want to talk about?" Raven asked, her gorgeous brown eyes fixed on him, almost daring him to close the subject and prove he didn't trust her.

"Her mother is my sister."

"Casey?"

"Yes."

"She wasn't married, I take it."

"No, she wasn't. The baby's father sweet-talked her out of her entire trust fund then beat her half to death when she wised up and tried to leave him—by then she was pregnant. It's amazing she didn't lose the baby."

"Oh, Matthew. I'm so sorry to hear that. How is she now?"

"Honestly? She's brain-damaged. Mentally she's about Jamie's age."

"He beat her that badly? Did he go to jail for it?"

"He went to jail for other things."

"I'm guessing the judge revoked his parental rights?"

"A judge didn't have to. Ray gave up his parental rights more than willingly. Signed Jamie over to me legally."

"How is it that the press didn't make a big deal about this? Jamie has to be around six or seven at least."

"She's eight. And the reason no one knows about her is because I've purposely kept a low profile. Remember we're just wrapping up the primary season. If I had continued on to the general election, I'm sure it would have come up."

She clamped her lips together as though purposely keeping her mouth shut. But Matthew saw the unasked questions lingering in her eyes. He didn't blame her. He supposed she instinctively formed the right questions in her mind. And that's what made her so good at her job. But reporter or no, to her credit she didn't pry.

"So tell me about your family. How's your dad?"

Raven's face clouded.

"What is it? Is he all right?"

"Oh, just a little high blood pressure and a fiancée who doesn't help it." She gave him a dubious grin. "Other than that, he's all right."

"Then why the long face?"

"Long face?"

"During our…previous acquaintance…your face lit up like a light show any time you mentioned your dad. The wonderful and wise Mac Mahoney. No one measured up, and, quite frankly, I was a little jealous."

A throaty laugh lifted into the air between them. "Believe me, Mac is still wonderful and wise. But let's just say I'm a little wiser as well."

"That's nice and cryptic of you."

She shrugged, her face hardening. "Not cryptic, just not a topic open for discussion."

"I see. You want your 'friends' to open up their family drama, but you're not willing to do the same. Typical."

"Oh, please. Don't try to turn this around on me."

"Would you like dessert?" The waiter's sudden appearance gave Matthew a start.

"No, thank you," Raven snapped. "I'd like the check please."

"*I'd* like the check," Matthew corrected, eyeing the waiter sternly.

"Don't you dare give it to him!"

"Shall I split it between you?" the waiter asked, his expression that of a deer caught in headlights.

"Yes, we'll go Dutch."

Matthew released an exasperated sigh. "Fine," he said to the waiter. "Split the check."

Smoke curled into the air from the cigarette clenched between his lips. He leaned against his car and watched the couple coming out of the restaurant across the street. Brief panic grabbed his stomach as the man hesitated, glanced toward him.

In a fit of daring, he'd parked right below the streetlight, which illuminated his blue hood. Now he had to wonder how smart it was to be parked where they might glance over and see him any second. But if Matthew Strong noticed a man leaning against an old blue beater, smoking a cigarette, he made no indication of it. Typical of a politician. Unless there were a baby he could kiss or a cause he could exploit, he wouldn't take notice of anything past the end of his own nose.

Raven Mahoney glanced at her watch impatiently, waiting for the valet to bring her car around. Her sleek black hair swayed with the jerky movements that clearly stated her irritation.

He'd recognize her anywhere. Even in the misty night, he could see her beauty every bit as defined as on television.

He took a long, slow drag from his cigarette and watched as a champagne-colored luxury car approached. The politician exchanged what was presumably a tip, for his keys. He opened the door to Raven's car for her and she slid not-so-gracefully inside.

They drove away, leaving him to stare until the taillights vanished from his view. After one last drag from his cigarette, he tossed it to the ground and headed for the driver's-side door.

Anger burned in him. But now wasn't the time for a confrontation. That would come later. After everything was in place.

Chapter Five

Standing on the darkened front porch, Raven fumbled with her keys, wishing she'd had the forethought to leave her front light on before rushing out to meet Ken earlier. But she'd been too focused on Matthew's story to worry about minor details. Minor at the time anyway. At this particular moment, darkness was of the utmost importance. The darkness always unnerved her.

Through the door, she could hear the phone ringing, and though she knew she had not only an answering machine, but also caller ID, she couldn't shake that feeling of not getting somewhere fast enough. Like being the heroine in a horror flick, who can't find the right key to her car ignition, and the window is open and the maniac gets there just as she speeds off. Sometimes it's too late, and sometimes it's not.

Raven shuddered at the thought. She finally located the proper key and slid it into the lock. Relief flowed through her as she opened the door, then closed it firmly behind her.

Movement to her left gave her a start. She jumped and squealed. Then she recognized her reflection in the foyer mirror. With a chuckle she shook her head, feeling like a complete idiot for being so spooked.

Walking into the kitchen, she took a glance at the caller ID and frowned at the private caller message. She checked out the answering machine. No flashing light. No messages.

"Oh, well," she said to Ginger, the fat stuffed tabby cat perched on her special chair against the kitchen bar. "I guess if it's important enough, they'll call back."

The phone rang. She rubbed her hand along Ginger's fake fur and grinned. "See?"

She grabbed the phone and pressed the button. "Hello?"

"Did you forget about our dinner?"

Anxiety slammed into Raven at the sound of the vaguely familiar voice. "Who is this?" she demanded, drawing on every ounce of bravado she possessed.

"Sonny."

Inwardly, she groaned. How on earth could she have forgotten about meeting her brother, for crying out loud?

"Oh, Sonny! I'm so sorry. I can't believe I did that. I was doing some research on a story."

Silence loomed on the other end of the line and Raven frowned. "Sonny? Are you still there?"

"Yeah, I'm still here. It's okay. Don't worry about it. Hang on, I have another call."

Raven walked across the kitchen floor, carrying the cordless next to her ear. She opened the refrigerator and went on the prowl. After eating barely half of her way-too-expensive meal, she was starving, but the sudden need to fill her stomach put her too closely in mind of the emotional void she'd also been trying to satiate. She closed the door.

Only pizza would do at a time like this.

"Okay, I'm back."

"Listen, Sonny, I feel horrible about wigging out like that. Can I make it up to you?"

"Sure you can."

Raven expelled a relieved breath as she recognized the lift in his tone.

"Great. How about tomorrow at lunch? We could meet at the deli on the corner of Fremont and Grand."

"You sure you won't forget during a workday?"

"I'm sure." Raven had to smile a little. He sounded almost like a wary child. "And it's my treat. The least I can do after forgetting our dinner tonight."

"Okay. I'll see you then."

Raven disconnected the call and snatched Ginger from her stool next to the kitchen bar. With the phone in one hand and the toy in the other she padded into the living room and plopped onto the overstuffed sofa.

"Memory one." She sighed, pressing the button. "A girl really shouldn't have the local pizza joint programmed into her phone," she told Ginger. "It's creepy."

Almost as creepy as talking to a one-eyed stuffed animal.

After placing her order, Raven hit the shower, emerging fifteen minutes later still exhausted from lack of sleep, but good for at least another hour. She stretched out on the sofa to wait for the pizza guy and relived every second since she'd laid eyes on Matt at the gym.

He was still the only man alive who had the power to make her palms sweat. Sitting across from him at dinner had taken her back fifteen years.

As memories flowed in, she leaned her head against the arm rest and allowed herself a brief moment of regret and what-ifs, visions of a different path. After fif-

teen years of staunchly refusing to allow herself a look
into an alternate life reality, Raven knew she was treading dangerous waters with this look-see, but she
couldn't keep the dreams from crashing in waves upon
the shores of her mind.

By the time her doorbell rang fifteen minutes later,
she and Matthew were married with three kids and living in the White House. The perfect First Family. She
stretched and smiled at the image, but at the insistent
ringing of the bell, she shook herself from the dream.

Two slices of stuffed-crust pepperoni pizza later, and
two full glasses of filtered water, and she was ready to
hit the sack.

She stretched out onto her bed, but sleep eluded her
as she realized she may have blown it with Matthew tonight by getting so testy. But opening up was difficult.
In a perfect world, her emotional baggage wouldn't be
an issue. In reality, opening up even for the wrong reasons—like lulling him into a false sense of security in
order to weasel a story out of him—was way too risky.
Her heart just wasn't up to it.

Frustration forced the door closed a little harder than
Matthew intended and shook the crystal chandelier
hanging in the expansive foyer.

"Whoa there, champ. Might want to ease up on those
bench presses or I won't have my handcrafted Louis
XIV–style door for long."

Matthew tossed his mother an apologetic smile.
"Sorry."

She rose on her tiptoes and pressed a kiss to his
cheek. The familiar smell of her perfume touched his
senses and he began to relax.

"Come into the kitchen and I'll make you a cup of

chamomile tea," she said, "Then you can tell me what happened at the gym that has you so upset."

He followed her into the spacious kitchen that gleamed with stainless-steel appliances and fluorescent lighting. The room might have seemed cold if not for his mother's warm presence.

Matthew sat at the kitchen table and watched her graceful movements as she prepared their tea. Childhood memories wafted over his mind.

"You were the reason Dad was such a success, weren't you?"

She glanced at him over her shoulder, a bewildered frown creasing her brow. "Whatever made you think such a thing?"

He shrugged. "I don't know. Just remembering all the public appearances where you stood at his side, smiling, supporting him. Supporting him at home and still taking time for Casey and me."

She turned, carrying two steaming cups on delicate saucers. Regret covered her features. "I could have done better. If I'd spent more time with your sister, maybe she wouldn't have…"

She set the saucers on the table and sank into her own chair. Her faded blue eyes wandered past him to stare at the wall. "I think sometimes your father and I will have to answer to God for our children's unhappiness."

"Unhappiness? Mom, I had a great childhood. So did Casey."

"Happy children turn into happy adults, my boy." She patted his hand wistfully.

"And I am happy."

With a dubious lift of her eyebrows, she sipped her tea. "No, you are not."

Matthew scowled. "I suppose it depends on your definition of *happy*, then. Because I have a full life. A wonderful mother who loves and supports me, a kid I couldn't live without."

"No career, a sister who can barely remember her own name, and loneliness."

Matthew couldn't help but grin. "And with that last point, you mean to bring up the well-worn subject of my marital status."

Her chin rose with dignity. "It bears repeating. You need a wife."

Yes, he certainly did. But not just any wife would do. And nothing had driven that fact home more than his date this evening. If you could call it that.

"Well, we won't belabor the point," his mother said. "Tell me what happened tonight to upset you."

Matthew hesitated. Did he really want to let his mother in on the fact that he'd spent the evening with Raven Mahoney? But almost before he could decide on his own, the words spilled from his mouth. "I had dinner with Raven."

"That Mahoney girl from so long ago?" Surprise combined with disapproval flashed in her expressive eyes.

"One and the same." Matthew sipped his tea.

"You don't learn your lessons very well do you? Are you going to have to go around this same mountain twice?"

"Raven's hardly a 'lesson' or a 'mountain,' Mother. We had dinner. Period. And to be honest, that's why I am so frustrated. It didn't go very well."

At her look of satisfaction, irritation nipped at Matthew's heart. "Don't look so pleased, Mother."

Her expression suddenly went bland. "I'm sorry, son, but a mother can't help but hold a bit of resentment against the girl who broke her wonderful son's heart."

"I appreciate the loyalty," he drawled.

"Don't be sarcastic. What did she do this time that has you in such a bad mood?"

"Nothing, really. She's just as closed up as ever." He fingered the rim of his cup. "I told her about Jamie, but she still couldn't open up." And then there was that awkward moment when she hesitated to pray at dinner. Had her relationship with God cooled over the years?

"Oh, Matt, really. The girl is a reporter. Are you so blinded you can't see why she would contact you out of the blue?"

Stung, Matthew scowled. "What makes you think I didn't call her?"

His mother raised that one eyebrow the way she did every time she had a point to make. "Did you?"

"No."

Her eyes softened. "Son. Don't be duped into giving away our family secrets."

"I'm afraid Ray is going to do it anyway."

"Ray? What do you mean?"

A heavy sigh escaped him. "I didn't tell you quite everything. He's threatening to go to the press."

She gave a dismissive wave of her thin, vein-lined hand. "Oh, pooh. Public records show Jamie is adopted and that her birth mother is your sister. There's nothing new for him to tell." She frowned as though realization dawned. "What did he threaten to make you pull out of the race? And don't tell me you just decided it wasn't the direction you wanted your life to take, after all. I want the truth."

"I gave him ten thousand dollars to stay away from Casey and Jamie."

"Matthew Strong! We do not give in to extortion!" His mother's eyes flashed fire.

"There was more to it than that. He threatened to go to the press and claim we forced him to sign away his rights to Jamie."

"Preposterous! He was only more than happy to do that in exchange for his legal fees. He doesn't care anything about Jamie. We should have let that monster deal with a public defender. He'd still be in prison!"

"Preposterous or not, his claims would be believed by some. And if some advocate's group gets hold of his case, we could be taking a chance on losing my daughter. I'd rather pay the money."

"And lose your career?"

"Yes. Who is really going to care about his claims if I'm a nobody?"

She stood and walked around to his side of the table. After pressing a kiss to his head, she looked firmly into his eyes with fierce love. "You'll never be a nobody, Matt. You were destined for greatness."

He gave a short laugh. "Greatness has eluded me, Mother. I'll settle for being a great dad."

"You're already a great dad. And I didn't necessarily mean you'll be great in politics. Although you most certainly would have been as great as your father. Any man willing to set aside his dreams in order to protect his child is worthy of admiration. I'm proud of you."

Matthew stood and pushed in his chair. He snatched his mother around the shoulders and gave her a squeeze before letting her go. "I'm not sure I deserve that pride. But it feels good to know I have it."

"Always." She smiled and nodded toward the kitchen door. "Jamie is reading before bed. I suggest you go upstairs and say goodnight before she falls asleep."

As he ascended the stairs, Matthew's heart lifted at the thought of spending a few moments alone with

Jamie. At the end of a long, disappointing day, Jamie was a bright light. An oasis.

The soft glow of a lamp greeted him as he walked into a room decorated with baseball wallpaper and bedspread. St. Louis Cardinals' keepsakes plastered every spare corner. The girl was obsessed with the sport, much to her grandmother's chagrin.

He stood at the door and watched her for a second before she noticed him. A smile lifted the corners of his lips at the sight of his daughter lying in bed, covered to her armpits and wearing a Cardinals' cap. She looked up and her face brightened. "Hey, Dad. Where've you been? We ate without you."

"I ate out."

A teasing glint rose in her eyes. "With a girl?"

"That's my business," he said, ruffling the girl's blond hair. "What are you reading?"

"Lord of the Rings."

Matthew nodded his approval and sat down at the side of the bed. "How do you like it?"

Jamie shrugged. "Movie's better."

At eight years old, Jamie picked up everything she could get her hands on. Matthew loved that about her, but admittedly, *Lord of the Rings* might be a bit much for a kid who had only been reading alone for two years. "Naw, the movie's easier, but not better."

"I think it's better," she insisted.

"Oh, well. What do you know?" He grinned and tweaked her nose. "You're just a kid."

"Aunt Casey knew me today."

"She did?" Mom hadn't told him. Casey had good days and bad, and although Jamie knew Casey was her mother biologically, she'd always called her "Aunt Casey." Everyone had agreed it would be easier that way.

"What did you two do?"

"We played Memory. I won."

"Did you cheat?"

She shrugged. "Not much."

Matthew bit back a grin. The girl was almost too honest. "Jamie, it's not nice to cheat."

"I said I didn't do it much."

"You shouldn't have done it at all."

She heaved a sigh and set her book down. "Sorry."

"We'll let it go this time. But don't do it again. It's not fair to Aunt Casey. You'd probably win anyway. You don't need to cheat."

"I know, but sometimes I can't help myself."

"Work on that."

"Okay, I will."

"Ready to say your prayers?" Matthew pushed back the comforter to reveal the rest of his pajama-clad daughter. She swung her skinny legs over the side of the bed and knelt beside him.

"Take off the cap," Matthew said.

He listened to her say her prayers, the sweet fragrance of fellowship wafting to heaven from the precious lips of his little girl. She was worth every sacrifice he could have possibly made to insure her safety and peace of mind.

Father, I know You love her even more than I ever could. Help me to keep her safe.

Chapter Six

Raven glanced around the crowded deli. She wasn't sure who to look for, but somehow, she found herself seeking out anyone who might resemble her—to explain her own dark hair and brown eyes when her sisters, with their red hair and fair complexions, clearly favored their mother.

Several single—or at least sitting alone—men caught her attention, but smoldering eyes and seductive smiles clearly relayed less than brotherly intentions. Finally, after several minutes of futile searching for Sonny, Raven found an empty booth and plopped down.

She *was* five minutes early after all. Sonny might be the kind of person who had on-the-dot punctuality. Although, truthfully, she couldn't imagine any brother of hers possessing such a quality—or flaw, depending on how you looked at it.

The waitress strolled by and set a glass of water in front of her.

"Thanks," Raven said. She smiled, ever conscious of her public image, despite Ken's perpetual insistence that she flattered herself when she thought anyone recognized her. So maybe her station was a small cable network, not some big network affiliate, but there *were* viewers, Mac and her sisters, to name a few, otherwise they wouldn't be on the air.

"What can I get you today?" the waitress asked, friendly, but obviously rushed.

"Nothing just yet. I'm waiting for someone."

The waitress sighed. "All right. I'll check back when I see two heads instead of one."

Raven smiled again. "Thanks."

She waited twenty more minutes, watching as the crowd ebbed and flowed, endlessly repopulated by different faces. Glancing at her watch, she realized she wasn't going to have time to eat before getting back to work. She snatched a couple of dollars out of her purse and tossed them on the table. No sense in the server losing out on a tip just because she'd been stood up.

Just as she walked outside into the fresh summer breeze, her phone beeped. Anticipating Sonny's apology or excuses, she snatched it from her purse and answered with a clipped hello.

"Hey, how'd you know it was me?" asked the male voice on the other end of the line.

"Who is this? Sonny?"

"Sonny? Ah, so you're annoyed with someone else."

Matthew. Now there was a surprise. Raven had planned to give him a couple of days to forget her bad manners, then she was going to call him to apologize.

"Why did you think I knew who you were?"

"I didn't figure you'd bark at anyone but me after last night."

"I didn't exactly bark," she said. "I just…got stood up for a lunch date and now I'll be starving all afternoon."

"Why didn't you just order something to go?"

"No time."

A pregnant pause filled the lines. "All right, I'll get to the point. Have you ever been kayaking?"

"Kayaking?"

"Yeah, little boat on the water? You know."

"I know what kayaking is…but no I've never gone. We just use plain fishing boats in the river back home."

"Well, I thought I'd get away this weekend and do some white-water kayaking. Want to come with me?"

Raven swallowed hard. After the way she had treated him, he was asking her out? "I… Hey, how did you get my number anyway?"

"I called the station."

"And they gave you my cell phone number?" Outraged, Raven made a mental note to make some heads roll as soon as she made it back to work.

"I asked for you, told them who I was and they connected me to some guy."

"What was this guy's name? Do you remember?"

"Ken."

"That explains it."

"What?"

"Ken is my camera guy. He probably smells a story."

"I see."

"Don't worry about him," Raven said quickly, feeling him withdraw from her.

"No, I know. So what do you say?"

"I guess I could take a Saturday off to do some kayaking."

"Great. Can I pick you up around eight?"

"Sure. Do you need my address?"

"I have it."

"Let me guess, Ken gave you that too?"

His low chuckle tickled her ear and quickened her pulse.

She cleared her throat to steady her nerves. "All right. Pick me up on Saturday then. I'll be ready at eight."

"Great. Bye."

Raven flipped the top of her phone down to disconnect. She hurried to her car and made it to the station just in time to be blindsided by Kellie Cruise's ten-thousand-dollar smile, sparkling with overblown wattage from behind the anchor desk.

Anxiety gripped her stomach. "What is she doing?" Raven whispered in Ken's ear.

"They took Bruce to the hospital a half hour ago. He was complaining of chest pains."

"Why didn't you call me? I should be up there, not her!"

"Frank asked for you first. You should have been here."

Raven threw him a dirty look.

"Hey, come on," he said. "Frank said you were to go look into that robbery at Commerce Bank. We might as well get that done."

With one last glance at the girl who was slowly inching her way into *her* position, Raven followed Ken through the hallway, and out the door.

"All right. Let's go." She scowled. "Oh, by the way. What's the big idea giving out my cell phone number and address?"

He gave her a Cheshire-cat grin. "I take it your boyfriend got in touch?"

"First of all…he's not my boyfriend. Second of all…stick to the point. Where's your professional courtesy? We do not give out colleagues' numbers, no matter what."

A look of mock regret passed over his lined features.

"Oh, wow. I didn't know that. It'll never happen again. Scout's honor."

Raven rolled her eyes at him over the hood of the SUV. "You're no scout and you have no honor."

"I'm hurt. Really hurt."

"Sure you are. Just get in and let's get this stupid robbery story over with."

Raven walked out of the station later than usual that night. The bank robbery story had actually turned out to be a good one, and as much as she hated the idea that a serial bank robber was on the loose, this sort of report, which played on the fears of depositors, kept people tuned in. She'd earned a big thumbs-up from the news director, which was extremely gratifying. But better yet, in the midst of the nightly news report, Kellie had mispronounced the word *incumbent* with a long *u*. Of course, off air, she'd been a laughingstock, and though Raven hadn't joined in with the hecklers, she'd nevertheless felt a broad sense of satisfaction.

She smiled as she headed for her car. Footsteps on the pavement behind her alerted her senses and she tensed, quickening her own steps. By the time she reached her SUV, her heart was pounding furiously and adrenaline rushed through her veins. Grateful for keyless entry, she pressed the button and reached for her handle.

A hand gripped her shoulder. "Raven, wait."

She sprang into survival mode. Whipping around, she drew on her self-defense training, used her knee, and with the heel of her hand she was about to connect with her assailant's chin when she recognized her so-called attacker.

"Matt!" she gasped. "For crying out loud, what are you doing?"

He scowled from a bent-over position, obviously trying to recover his breath, if not dignity.

Raven frowned. "Are you okay?"

He straightened and lifted a bag from the ground where it had fallen. He handed it out. "I brought you supper."

"You did?"

He nodded. "I knew you missed lunch and when I talked to Ken a couple of hours ago, he told me you hadn't eaten supper either."

Ken was really pushing this story. She couldn't blame him, really. And admittedly, seeing Matt brought her a sense of joy she was nowhere near ready to try to analyze.

"I'm sorry if I hurt you."

He shrugged and a sheepish grin showed beneath the glow of the pole lights spaced throughout the parking lot. "I should have called out to let you know it was me, but I was trying to decide what might scare you more. Guess I called it wrong."

"Yeah, sneaking up on someone with slightly paranoid tendencies in the first place isn't necessarily a good idea."

"I'll remember that in the future."

Somehow, the way he said *future* sent a shiver of pleasant possibility down Raven's spine. She held up the bag. "What'd you get me?"

"What else?" His grin nearly sent her heart into a tailspin.

"Egg drop soup, extra crunchy noodles, and two egg rolls?"

He nodded.

"I can't believe you remember."

She held her breath as he took a step closer.

"I remember everything."

"Like what?" She knew she was walking into volatile emotional territory, but couldn't resist the heady feeling his closeness evoked. She leaned back against her door. He reached forward and rested his arm just above her head.

"I remember that you like hot chocolate in the summer and iced tea in the winter."

"I—I guess I'm weird."

"Unique," he soothed.

How in the world did this man have the power to make her feel as though she was the only woman in the world?

"That's not all I remember."

"What else?" she whispered.

His gaze searched hers. His thumb pressed against her lips. "I remember how your mouth quivers when you know I'm about to kiss you."

"I-it does?" Paralyzed, she felt herself being pulled into the heady depths of the promise in his eyes.

He nodded as his head descended. Raven relaxed against him at the first, warm feel of his lips on hers. He deepened their kiss and she clung to him. Headlights pulled into the parking lot, then out again. But the distraction was enough to bring them to their senses. Matthew pulled back, leaving Raven's head spinning and her breath short, leaving her desperate to press her mouth to his for one more kiss before they said goodbye for the evening.

"I guess I'm getting ahead of myself," he said, his husky voice telling her more than words ever could. "It just feels like we're taking up where we left off."

Raven nodded her agreement. "I know what you mean. But it isn't smart to move too quickly."

"I promise to keep my distance." He grinned. "At least until I see you again."

A short laugh escaped Raven. "That's reassuring." But it wasn't reassuring. The thought disturbed her. How would Matt feel when he discovered her reason for seeing him again?

Any girl who could double over a guy like Matthew Strong had to be able to take care of herself. He'd have to remember that in case he needed the information later on. Under cover of darkness he watched them.

The kiss was a surprise. First of all, Matthew was religious, so who knew he'd move so fast? And Raven Mahoney had kissed him back without a fight. A surprise for a girl with such an air of aloof inapproachability.

Then it occurred to him. These two had a history.

Matthew held the door and Raven got inside her SUV. As he watched Matthew stride across the parking lot to his own car, he digested this new scenario he hadn't anticipated. Would he have to split them apart? Or could he use the relationship to his advantage?

Matthew pulled out of the parking lot, his heart light, downright giddy. He glanced at the city lights, wondering what he should do next. One thing was for certain, going home was no option. Too much adrenaline rushed through him to settle in for the night. He'd already tucked Jamie into bed before he left the house, so she'd be down for the count, otherwise he'd see if she was up for a game of night basketball.

He was a little disappointed that Raven hadn't invited him to share dinner with her, but he supposed she needed to process what had happened between them. Possibility spurred a sense of hope inside him. What if they had a future together after all? He placed a quick call to let his mother know not to wait up.

Ten minutes later, he swung the Lexus into the parking lot of Randy's Gym and killed the motor. He grabbed his workout bag from the back seat and headed into the all-but-deserted gym.

He changed in the locker room then made a beeline for the treadmill, his legs warming in anticipation of a good run.

A hint of rain scented the air by the time he left the building. He breathed in deeply, feeling refreshed, relaxed and ready to go home and crawl into bed.

"Matthew, is that you?"

He started at the sound of a feminine voice and turned.

A petite young woman stood before him, smiling brightly.

Matthew waited for her to speak. When she didn't, he gave her a tentative smile. "Yes?"

Her smile turned to a pout. "You mean you don't recognize me?"

The pout gave it away. "Kellie? Good grief, when did you grow up?"

She gave a throaty, not-so-little-girlish laugh. "I've been grown up for a while. And if you ever attended my mother's parties with your mother, you'd have known that."

He gave an exaggerated shudder. "Dinner parties. Please. I only attend when I must."

"Yes, but look what you're missing out on." She gave a flirty little spin and was laughing when she faced him a split second later.

Amusement filled him and he smiled at the child. No, not really a child anymore. "You're quite the young lady now. I'm sorry I didn't recognize you."

"Oh, that's all right. My heart can take it." She

stepped closer. "You—uh—know I'm working for Daddy now, right?"

"At the station?"

"Yes. I graduated with my degree in broadcast journalism."

"So you're a reporter." Now, he understood her sudden appearance. "Nice try." He tweaked her nose as though she were still the fifteen-year-old he remembered. "How'd you really know I was here?"

A pretty pout found its way to her lips. "I saw you talking to Raven Mahoney."

He couldn't quite contain his amusement. "You followed me and waited for two hours for me to come out?"

"Yes. That's what good reporters do."

"You could have just called the house. I would have turned you down over the phone without you having to wait for nothing."

"Come on, Matt. How about throwing me a bone here? It'll make my career."

He gave a conciliatory smile. "You don't need me. Sounds like you have your dad to make your career for you already."

She squared her shoulders and a deep frown formed a *V* in her forehead, diminishing her pixieish charm. "I'm working as hard as anyone else. I deserve a promotion just as much as…" She gathered a long breath. "Oh, never mind. It doesn't matter. But don't think just because Daddy got me the job, that I'm coasting by."

Matthew held up his hands in surrender. "I wasn't implying you don't work hard. I'm happy that you like your job."

"But no quote?"

"Sorry, you'll just have to get that promotion on your own."

She scowled. "If Raven doesn't steal it out from under me."

"Raven?"

She scowled. "Yes, *Raven*."

"What's she got to do with your promotion?"

She opened her car door and slid under the wheel. "Your sexy little ex-y and I are up for the same anchor job. So don't be fooled if she acts like she wants to re-kindle an old flame. It was nice seeing you again." She handed him a card. "Take this and call if you change your mind."

Unease crept into Matthew's gut as drove home. Was Raven's re-entry into his life too convenient to be coincidence?

Chapter Seven

Her favorite late-night talk show wasn't particularly funny this evening.

"Get some new material," Raven grouched. She snatched up the remote and flipped from channel to channel trying to find something, anything to keep her thoughts from reliving that world-shattering kiss a thousand more times.

Why hadn't she invited him over to help her eat the Chinese takeout? He'd gotten enough for two, as he always had during their college years. Guilt plagued her. That was why. She knew a relationship was the last thing she intended to pursue with her old flame. Knew that in all likelihood he was still in love with her. But, her own feelings notwithstanding, she just had too much baggage to attempt anything resembling commitment. And part of that baggage included her desperate need to get this anchor spot.

She snatched up the phone and dialed Denni's number. She knew her sister was barely back from her Hawaiian honeymoon, but she had the rest of her life to snuggle with her hunky cop husband, Reece Corrigan.

"Aloha! Mrs. Corrigan speaking." The pure joy in Denni's voice sent a jolt of warmth through Raven and a smile touched her lips without warning.

"Aloha yourself, Mrs. Corrigan. Is that the way you answer all your calls now?"

Denni laughed. "Caller ID. I knew it was you."

"Oh, duh. I wonder if there's anything in the Constitution about privacy that we could bring up to ban caller ID. Talk about your lack of privacy."

"Only if you're a stalker, telemarketer or bill collector. Otherwise you're going to want the person you're calling to know who you are anyway."

"Oh philosophical one, marriage must be making you think deeply."

"Marriage is wonderful." Denni gave a sigh and Raven's heart clenched. This time with just a twinge of longing. "Hawaii is definitely paradise."

"Reece didn't run off with a hula girl, I guess."

"No way," a male voice piped in. "I only have eyes for one woman."

"Denni! I'm on speaker?"

"Sorry, I was unpacking."

Raven heard a click. "All right. I'm all yours. I'm walking down the hall to my little office and you can tell me why you're really calling."

"Oh, just to see how you've been." Raven cringed. Good thing she hadn't dreamed of being an actress, because she couldn't act her way out of a paper bag.

"What's wrong, Rave?" Denni's sympathetic tone forced sudden tears to Raven's eyes.

"I've been seeing Matt again."

"Matthew Strong?"

"Who else?"

"Raven, that's great. I never thought you were over him in the first place."

The rush of matrimonial bliss in Denni's tone grated on Raven. Especially when romantic feelings had nothing to do with anything in this situation.

"Well, it's not quite like that."

"What do you…?" A gasp shot through the line with all the indignation of a woman in love. "Raven, you are *not* playing with that poor man's heart just to get a story!"

"Don't be absurd." Raven winced. There was that bad acting again.

"You *are*. Oh, Rave. That's low even for you."

"*Even* for me?" What an assessment from her own sister.

"Don't pretend to be offended by that. You are the one who says the end always justifies the means and usually you don't cross the line too much, but this is just wrong. You broke Matt's heart fifteen years ago and now you want to get his hopes up and break it all over again?"

"Hey, I have feelings too, ya know."

Raven pushed up from the couch, grabbed Ginger and padded toward the bedroom.

"Are your feelings getting involved here, Raven?" Denni's point-blank question shot through Raven as she flopped onto her stomach across her bed, resting on her elbows.

"How could they not? You know how much he meant to me."

"Yes, I do." She spoke softly, in true Denni fashion. Now was the time for her to stop and listen to whatever Raven had to say, to help her find her own answer to whatever problem she might be facing. Only, Raven didn't know what to say.

"Raven, are you still in love with Matt?"

A deep sigh welled up within her and she blew it out in a cleansing breath. "I am. Yes. Wow, I can't believe I just said that."

Denni laughed. "You have to tell him."

"Oh, Denni. I can't. I don't know if I'm ready for a relationship."

"What are you afraid of? What happened between the two of you back then that was so awful you couldn't work it out?"

"I—I can't tell you. I wish I could and I probably will some day soon. But not yet. Okay?"

"All right. But promise me you'll give up this story about Matt."

"I would if I could just find something else to knock out of the park so Mr. Cruise will give me that anchor job and not his perky little daughter."

"You will. I'll pray for just the most awesome story ever."

Raven frowned. She had pushed her childhood faith so far into the depths of her being that when her family brought up religion, it always filled her with bittersweetness.

Memories of church services, singing, clapping, listening with awe as Mama sang "'Tis So Sweet to Trust in Jesus." Raven wanted to trust. She did, but how could she trust when everything she knew about who she was turned out to be a lie?

"If you want to wish me luck, I'll take it," she blurted into the mouthpiece. "But save your prayers. They mean nothing to me."

Denni paused only for a second. "They may not mean anything to you," she said, with no condemnation in her tone. "But they mean something to God."

"Believe that if it makes you feel better, Denni. Believe that there is some great big Daddy Warbucks in the sky just waiting to give me a great news story, but I'm not going to hold my breath."

"Fine. Have you heard from Dad, lately?"

"I've had a couple of messages from him, but I haven't had time to call him back."

A frustrated sigh reached her ears. "Raven. What's it going to hurt for you to call him?"

"I've been busy all week."

A beep indicated another caller. "Hang on a sec. I'm getting another call."

"Hello?"

A pause.

"Hello?"

"Where were you today?"

"Who is this?"

"Sonny."

"What do you mean, where was I? I was at the deli we agreed upon. I waited for twenty-five stinking minutes and missed lunch while you stood me up, so don't ask where I was. Where were you?"

He chuckled and she could hear the crackle as he took a drag on a cigarette. "Got quite the temper. I guess you come by that naturally enough."

"Sorry. It's been a long day."

"No problem. We must have gotten our delis mixed up. Can we try again this weekend?"

"I'm sorry, Sonny. I have plans for the weekend."

"Plans?" His tone hardened. "What sort of plans?"

"Private ones."

"I see," came the clipped response. "I suppose we'll have to make it another time, then."

"I suppose. Call me next week and we'll set something up, okay?"

"Sure." He hung up without saying goodbye.

"Sheesh, talk about a temper," Raven muttered. She clicked the button to take her back to Denni. "Sorry, Den."

"Oh, hi. You're back." She giggled and in the background Raven could hear Reece's muffled voice.

Raven smiled. Reece wasn't the type of man to be kept waiting long. Apparently he'd tired of his wife yakking with her sister.

"I'll call you in a few days, Denni."

"All right. And Raven, give yourself a chance to love again. Seriously. Finding the love of your life is the most wonderful experience in the world."

Raven pictured Denni and Reece. She could imagine Denni looking deep into his eyes as she said those words. A lump lodged in Raven's throat. "Goodbye," she whispered.

The problem was that she had already found the love of her life. She had given him up. And now, with his re-emergence into her life, she faced a hard decision. If she wanted Matthew, she couldn't use him to get a story. The question was…which did she want more?

Fear shot through Matthew's heart as he stared at the letter in his hands. Ray Marx must have spent all of his money and was looking for more.

SHE'S MINE, NOT YOURS.

Capital letters, typewritten. No signature. How clichéd, and yet terrifying at the same time. Clearly, Ray was letting Matthew know that he wouldn't go away. No matter what.

Matthew shook his head. He knew one thing for sure.

He couldn't go to the river tomorrow with Raven and leave Jamie home. He'd be worried sick the entire time.

He and Raven hadn't spoken since the night he kissed her. After his encounter with Kellie, he wasn't sure what to say to Raven. His heart wasn't quite ready to believe she could pretend so well. He remembered what a lousy actress she was. Whatever her motives, her feelings were transparent. Another idea formed and he snatched up the phone. She answered on the first ring.

"Matt?"

"Hi. Change of plans for the weekend, do you mind?"

"No kayaking?" Her voice reflected a mix of relief and disappointment.

"I don't want to leave my daughter, but she hates kayaking. How about Adventure Park in St. Louis?"

"You…want me to meet your daughter? Are you sure?"

"I'll introduce you as an old college friend. She's only eight, so she's not going ask you to be her new mommy."

Raven laughed. "That's a relief. All right. Adventure Park it is. Want to get an earlier start since it's a four-hour drive?"

"Yeah, can you be ready at five-thirty?"

Raven groaned. "I better go home now and go to sleep."

Laughter rumbled in Matthew's chest as a surge of affection rushed through him. "It's only noon."

"Yes, but five-thirty comes really, really early."

He was still smiling when he hung up. Then his gaze drifted downward to the note on his desk. Anger burned through him once again. Ray might have no ammunition to hurt him politically, but the man was obviously threatening to try to make a court case.

Matthew seriously doubted any rational judge would

give a little girl over to the man who'd abused her mother, causing brain damage. A convicted felon on parole. But you never could tell. A judge with a score to settle with Matthew or possibly his father before him. A judge who didn't like Matthew's politics. As unlikely as it seemed, Matthew knew he might very well lose Jamie if Ray could find a judge who would believe the Strong family had bullied him into signing away his parental rights to the little girl.

"Hi, Dad." Jamie rushed in without knocking as usual. "Want to go swimming?"

"Sure. And guess what?"

"What?"

"I have a surprise for you."

Her beautiful blue eyes lit up. "What is it?"

"How would you like to go to Adventure Park tomorrow?"

A wide grin split her face, revealing a mouthful of part baby teeth, part grown up teeth. "You mean it? You really, really mean it?"

She flung her arms around his neck.

"Of course I mean it."

"Is Grams coming?"

"I don't really think Grams would like that sort of thing, do you? I mean can you imagine her on a roller coaster?"

Jamie giggled and shook her head. "It's just you and me, then? I can't wait! I'm going to go tell Aunt Casey!"

"Uh, wait, Jamie." He stopped her just before she could sprint to the door.

She stared back at him, a slight frown marring her perfect skin.

Matthew released a breath. "Actually, I've invited an old college friend to join us. Do you mind?"

"Oh. I didn't know you had any friends. What's his name?"

Heat warmed Matthew's ears. "To tell you the truth, he's a she. And *her* name is Raven Mahoney."

"You mean you've got a *girlfriend?*" The incredulity in her voice relayed much more than Matthew expected she might deduce.

"She's not a girlfriend. She's a friend."

"I can't believe you invited a girl." Jamie scowled. "What a joke. You just want me to meet her 'cause you like her."

"Young lady. You better watch your tone and words with me."

"Fine. But don't expect me to like her."

"You'd best be polite."

She scowled again. "I'll see what I can do. But I'm not making any promises."

"Jamie…I mean it. Raven means a lot to me."

"I knew she was your girlfriend."

"No, she isn't. But once upon a time we were going to be married."

Jamie's eyes grew large and round. "Why didn't you?"

He tweaked her nose, which was peeling from too much sun. "That, my girl, is my business."

Releasing a heavy sigh, she padded to the door. "You still going to swim with me?"

"Yes, let me go get my suit on. You going to be okay with meeting Raven?"

A shrug lifted her bony shoulders. "I'm getting used to the idea. Think she'll like the roller coasters, or is she going to scream and hold on to your arm like a sissy?"

Matthew grinned. "If I remember right, I'm the one who screams. She'll be telling me not to be a wimp."

Jamie dimpled. "Okay. Then I can probably put up with her for one day."

"Glad to hear it. I'll meet you by the pool." Matthew laughed as she walked out of the room. The girl was a little more savvy than he'd given her credit for.

Tomorrow should prove to be an interesting day.

Chapter Eight

Raven loved the predawn stillness. Sitting on the deck, she sipped a steaming mug of coffee and relished the simplicity of a silent world. A world where she could quiet her mind and just…breathe.

During times like this she could almost believe God was looking down on her—as though all she had to do was look up and she'd have his undivided attention. Maybe while the rest of the city slept, He'd concentrate on her for a change. The thought almost induced a prayer. But not quite.

Her watch alarm beeped, reminding her that if she wanted to look presentable in thirty minutes, she'd better get it in gear.

After a quick, steamy shower, she emerged, ready to face a day of gut-tightening fun rides, cotton candy and greasy pizza—all way too expensive, but in her experience, worth every penny.

A wave of unease washed over her at the thought of meeting Matt's daughter. What if the girl hated her? Worse yet, what if she adored her and wanted a new mommy? The thought sent Raven rushing to the kitchen for a bottle of water to moisten her suddenly parched throat.

Her phone chirped. She snatched it up. "Yes?"

"G'morning."

Her heart did a little dance at the sound of Matt's low timbre. "Good morning to you too. You standing me up?"

"No way. I just wanted to ask you to meet me outside. Jamie fell asleep on the way over and I don't want to leave her while I walk up to the door."

Affection surged through Raven at his protectiveness. What a great dad. "Sure. I'll be watching for you."

He chuckled. "Actually, we're just outside. I'm calling from my cell phone."

She pushed aside the curtain and spied his car in her drive. A smile tipped the corners of her lips at the shadowy figure in the driver's seat. "I'll be right there."

After a double-check of her face and hair in the hallway mirror, she snatched up her mini-backpack—the best replacement for a purse on an active day—then locked her door and joined Matthew.

His white-toothed smile found its way straight to her heart. "All set?" he asked.

Raven nodded and slid into the leather seat. Matthew formed the same heart-stopping figure in casual clothes that he did in an elegant suit. A pair of jeans and a pullover shaved a good five years off his appearance. Not that he needed it.

She closed the door, covering them in darkness. With care, Matthew backed out of the drive and turned the car toward the interstate.

"Thank you for being okay with a change in plans today. I just didn't want to leave her alone."

"It's okay. Really, I love amusement parks."

A snort from the back seat gained her attention and

she glanced over her shoulder. The little girl's eyes were closed, but twitching a little too much to be believable. By that cynical snort, Raven could only conclude that Matt's daughter was determined not to like her. And Raven had a pretty good idea why.

"Oh, sure," she said, with an airy wave of her hand. "Amusement parks are where I take all my boyfriends."

"Huh?" Matthew gave her a frown that clearly indicated he thought she'd lost her marbles. But that sort of look couldn't deter Raven Mahoney. The little girl in the back seat had to be taught a lesson right up front, or today would be very uncomfortable for Raven. And she had no intention of allowing that to happen.

"Especially the ones I plan to snag into marriage."

Matthew's scowl deepened. "What are you talking about?"

"Oh, Matt. Imagine us at the top of the Ferris wheel, locked in an embrace." She frowned and clucked her tongue. "'Course, I don't know what we'd do with your little girl while we're up there together. Oh, well. No matter. I'm sure we can find someone willing to sit with her. Or maybe we can just get a rope and tie her to a pole until our romantic ride is over."

An indignant gasp shot forward from the back seat. "If you're riding with my dad, so am I!"

"Oh, so you're awake. Thought so." Raven grinned and held out her hand. "I'm Raven. Nice to meet you."

Without moving a muscle, the little girl sized her up. "You knew I was faking?"

"I figured."

"How'd you know?"

Clearly, the child wanted to avoid making the same mistake twice.

"You fidgeted in your seat like you were having trouble sitting still, and your eyeballs were moving too much under your eyelids."

"Hmm." Finally, the little girl accepted Raven's hand. "Jamie. Named after my Gramps." She gave a little sigh. "He died when I was seven."

"Your Gramps was a great man. I liked him very much."

Jamie's eyes grew wide. "You knew him?"

"I did. A long time ago."

The little girl hesitated a minute, still sizing Raven up like a judge in a hog contest at the county fair. "My Dad said you almost married him." She leaned forward. "Why'd you call it off?"

Raven distinctly remembered Matt's promise to "introduce her as an old friend from college."

She glared at him. He gave a sheepish shrug, but his boyish grin didn't offer much apology. "Sorry. She forced it out of me. What can I say? I'm weak where the women I love are concerned."

The look accompanying his last statement made his underlying message quite clear, and Raven was glad the little girl in the back seat prevented any further exploration of the topic. The kid might come in handy after all if Raven wanted to stave off any sort of personal conversation while she was working on the story.

"So?" Jamie's childish impatience rang in her voice, reminding them she'd voiced a question and wouldn't be put off. "Why'd you break up with my dad?"

"Hey, sport." To Raven's relief, Matt interjected. "What's with the third degree? Give Raven a break, huh?"

Jamie shrugged. "Just wondering."

"My past relationship with Raven is between us."

"Okay." She shrugged and stared out the window. "But I figure she must not be very smart if she dumped you."

Raven laughed. She couldn't help herself. This kid was great. Spunky, way too smart and wise beyond her years.

Matt's frown deepened. "Jamie, we had a deal. Stop it, already, and apologize to Raven."

"Sorry." Yeah, right, she was sorry.

"Hey, no problem. You know what? You're right. I was a dope back then."

"Does that mean you want him back?" Jamie's tone was fierce, almost threatening and Raven wasn't sure if the little girl didn't want her back in Matt's life, or if she simply didn't want him to be hurt again.

"Jamie…" Matt's voice took on a new firmness. A stern parental tone that relayed to his daughter enough was enough.

Jamie released a little sigh and clammed up. Matthew reached across the seat and gave Raven's hand a squeeze. "Sorry about that. She promised to behave herself."

Raven relished the warmth of his fingers. How long had it been since she'd actually wanted to be touched by a man? "I enjoyed the mental stimulation. You'd be surprised how little challenge I get these days."

"Anyone want to play a game?" Jamie asked.

Matthew removed his hand from hers. Raven shifted slightly so she could look in the back seat without whiplash. "What kind of game?"

"License plates. You have to see how many different states you can find."

Raven nodded and scanned the back of the car in front of them. "Okay. I see Michigan."

"Hey! That doesn't count. I go first."

"Why do you get to?"

She gave a scowl and a breathed out a huff. "Youngest always goes first."

"Not where I come from. When I was growing up, I

always started the games, and I'm the oldest kid in my family."

Jamie gave her that wise beyond years look again. Then nodded. "Fine. Oldest goes first. How old are you?"

"Jamie!" Matt's face reddened.

Still loving the challenge, Raven waved off his protest. "No problem, Matt. It's not like you don't know my age, anyway," she said matter-of-factly before turning back to her worthy opponent. "Thirty-five. How old are you?"

"Eight."

"Well, then. I guess Michigan stands and I get a point."

"Nope." A smug grin tilted Jamie's baby-pink lips. "Dad's thirty-seven. So he gets first pick."

Matthew laughed outright. "Hey, don't drag me into this. You two can battle it out on your own."

"Come on, Dad."

"Nope. I'm driving. I need to concentrate."

"But you always play."

"Not this time."

"Well, then," Raven said, unable to withhold a smug grin of her own. "I guess as the oldest, I go first. Write down Michigan under my name and give me a point."

Releasing a heavy sigh, Jamie poised her pencil. "Fine. How do you spell it?"

Raven supplied the spelling and the game moved forward.

"Florida," Jamie said, writing as she spoke.

"Missouri."

"Missouri doesn't count."

"Why not?" Raven's competitive nature reared its ugly head.

"Because it's our state."

"Well, I don't see why that makes a difference."

A chuckle from Matt brought a flush of embarrassment to Raven's cheek. She stuck out her tongue in his direction then turned her attention back to her little nemesis.

"Okay, if my choice doesn't count, then I get to go again."

Jamie gave a huff. "Fine."

They played for the next thirty minutes. Until finally they exhausted their choices. Jamie won by two states, although Raven was highly suspicious that she hadn't actually spied a Hawaii license plate. But short of calling the little girl an out-and-out liar, she didn't figure she could do much about it.

Raven's soft snoring brought a smile to Matt's lips. Though Jamie was clearly impatient to arrive at Adventure Park, as far as he was concerned, they could stay like this forever. The rousing license-plate game had convinced him Jamie and Raven were two peas in a pod and as mother and daughter, there would be a conflict every day of their lives. Enough to provide Raven with all the "mental stimulation" she wanted until Jamie was at least twenty-one.

The thought of Raven sliding into the role didn't cause him any alarm. He had no intention of letting her walk out of his life again. He glanced at her, marveling at her sleep-softened features, longing to reach out and test the smoothness of her skin. But he stopped himself short of doing just that. Politics had taught him there was a time to move in and a time to step back and watch. Today was a step-back-and-watch kind of day. He wouldn't make a pass, wouldn't talk about the past—unless she brought it up—wouldn't do anything that might cause her to run away from him.

No matter her motives for reentering his life, Matthew knew she still cared for him. And though he had no intention of revealing the reasoning behind his withdrawal from the senate race, he didn't mind baiting her a little bit to keep her around long enough to fall in love again.

"There's the Ferris wheel. No it's not real—wait, yes it is!" Jamie's excited announcement jolted Matt from his thoughts. Raven shot up straight.

"What's wrong?"

"Nothing. Jamie just saw the Ferris wheel."

"It's eighteen stories high," the little girl exclaimed proudly. "You can see the whole park from up at the top. Can we ride that one first, Dad?"

Matthew's stomach turned at the thought. How many minutes did that ride last, anyway? At least most of the roller coasters and other gut-hurling rides were only a couple of minutes in duration. Ferris wheels were a different story. Eighteen stories of slow torture. He gave a little involuntary shudder.

Raven's sleep-husky voice emitted a low chuckle. "Still scared of heights?"

He sent her a self-deprecating grin and cut a glance her way. "Deathly."

She slipped her warm hand inside his and smiled. "Don't worry, I'll hold your hand."

"If anyone's holding his hand, it's gonna be me," came the voice of outrage from the back seat. "Did you two forget I'm the kid? You can't go off holding hands and leave me in a park with a million, jillion people hanging around."

Raven let go of his hand. "The kid's right," she mumbled. "I don't know what I was thinking."

A strong sense of satisfaction spread through Matt at her discomfiture. The fact that she'd let Jamie gain the upper hand on this one proved she was feeling things that unnerved her. That was a good thing for Matt. Maybe before this day was over she'd realize that things weren't finished between them. Maybe she'd be willing to open up and tell him what had happened to rattle her enough that she could walk away from the strongest love either had ever known. Maybe by the end of the day, she would abandon her goal to achieve an exclusive (if what Kellie had implied was true) and once again be the love of his life.

Hope burned in his heart.

Maybe.

Keeping at least two cars between them, he nevertheless remained close enough to watch the Strong car swing off the interstate and onto the exit ramp. He took a long drag of his cigarette and held his breath as smoke fill his lungs. With a calm sense of satisfaction he released the smoke and flipped on his blinker. These two were starting to annoy him. What was next—an engagement?

Now, he couldn't allow that to happen, could he? The senator and the reporter. An unlikely couple, but when he factored in the kid in the back seat, everything took on a whole new dynamic. They were more than just a couple on a date. The kid, the amusement park... One happy little family.

He watched as they found a parking place and swung into a spot close by. They got out and Matthew Strong took the little girl by the hand. As they walked toward the gate, Strong looked over the kid's head and smiled at Raven Mahoney. Not that he blamed the guy. Raven was a looker. Better-looking than any girl he'd ever seen.

Pulling in another drag of smoke, he seethed inwardly and kept his gaze riveted on his target. The three of them looked for all the world like a family. A family. A *family*.

No. He couldn't allow that.

Chapter Nine

High-pitched squeals permeated the sky one-hundred and ten feet above St. Louis as the Screeching Hawk rose to its maximum height, then dropped at a rate of sixty miles an hour.

Raven raised her arms, closed her eyes, and relished the danger, excitement, the feeling of being totally out of control. She fought the urge to stand up. To see if she could maintain her balance while the world sped by. Mentally, she knew it was an ignorant thought. Still she couldn't keep from picturing it…Raven Mahoney, the king of the world—or queen as the case may be.

She hadn't been on a roller coaster in at least fifteen years, not since the last time she and Matthew had gone to Worlds of Fun in Kansas City. They'd been dating only a few weeks back then. Old memories. Bittersweet.

Was that the reason Matt had chosen to drive four hours to Adventure Park rather than take his daughter to the more local amusement park?

Don't analyze this, Raven. But the thought had already started to needle at her, pricking her thought processes, the part of her that needed to probe, dig, get to the bottom of every issue, every story. That part of her had driven her to be an ace reporter. And she couldn't deny the part of her that had brought her success.

She could still picture her first day as a rookie reporter. Shaking in her boots, standing in front of an enormous metal desk. Jonesy's cluttered office—the tough-guy station manager, a hulking bear of a man, three hundred pounds of pure attitude, with a voice to match. She'd always joked to herself that he led a secret life as a mob heavy. *Pay attention to the little details. The things no one else considers very important. File everything away in the back of your mind and hang onto it, 'cause you never know when a little tidbit of information will make the difference between reporting the same garbage as every other reporter or standing out in a crowd. I can already tell you're gonna be the kind to make a few waves. Women are gonna hate you and men are gonna be scared to death of you.* Then he'd winked. *Now, go find some news to report, and don't you dare let me down.*

And she never had. That little bit of advice had proven to be the reason she moved up so quickly. She noticed everything. Like the blue car that had followed them all the way from Kansas City. The same type of car she'd seen three times during the past week. She figured it was probably another reporter, trying to scoop her. A smile touched her lips. But, as many had discovered before, she didn't scoop easily.

Too bad Jonesy had turned over his job to that little weasel, Frank Cruise—Kellie's dad. If Jonesy were still boss, Raven wouldn't be scrambling to take advantage of her former relationship with Matt just to land an anchor job that was rightfully hers in the first place. But Jonesy's size and eating habits had caught up with him five years ago and he'd suffered a heart attack. After by-pass surgery and a wife-enforced retirement, he'd dropped seventy-five pounds, and the last Raven heard, had finished a marathon in just over four hours. She was happy for him, even if it did make things harder for her.

The Screeching Hawk ride had lasted a little over two minutes and in that time Raven's emotions had dipped and spun just as much as the roller coaster. Now, melancholy swept over her. She didn't like change. Didn't like that Jonesy was gone, that Ken was flirting around with Kellie Cruise—whether his intention was simply to goad Raven into going after the story or not. She didn't like that Mac was getting so close to marrying the floozy from Texas or that both of her sisters were now married.

The ride came to a full stop and she glanced over at Matt. Affection surged through her at his white-knuckled grip on the bar.

"You can let go now," she said. "The ride's over."

"Can we go again?" Jamie asked.

Matthew cleared his throat. "Umm—let me just catch my breath before we make that decision."

Her expression crashed. "May I have some cotton candy?"

"Later." Matt's legs seemed about to fail him and Raven slipped her hand into the crook of his arm to steady him. "You okay?"

He nodded and gave her a sheepish grin. "I will be. But I have to tell you, I don't know how I'm going to survive the rest of today without becoming a complete disappointment to my daughter."

Raven laughed. "You can hold on to me. I'll keep you safe."

"Will you?" He stopped short, grabbed her hand and

gave her a look of such intensity that Raven drew a sharp breath.

"Are you guys coming?" Jamie's impatient voice preempted anything he might have said. "There's the cotton-candy machine."

Reluctance flickered in his eyes. Raven let out the breath she'd been holding as his attention rightfully switched to his little girl. "We're coming, James. And anyway, it's too early for cotton candy. We'll have lunch in a little while, *then* cotton candy."

Jamie kicked at the ground with her gym shoe. Her knobby knees, centered in thin, deeply tanned legs had more marks than Mac's old work table out at the cabin. "Hey, Jamie," Raven called on a whim.

"What?" The kid's tone mirrored her freckled scowl. Raven raised her eyebrows. Apparently the camaraderie of the license-plate game had faded.

Matthew flipped the bill of her baseball cap, knocking it off her head. "Watch your tone, young lady."

Jamie caught the cap before it could hit the ground. "Sorry," she murmured.

"It's okay," Raven replied graciously. "I was just wondering where you got all those scars on your legs."

"Lots of places." Jamie slipped her hand into Matthew's, turning her back and tugging her dad forward so that Raven was forced to walk behind.

"Like where?"

The little girl lifted her slim shoulders in a shrug. "Soccer, field hockey, baseball."

"I guess you like sports, huh?"

The girl tossed back a "duh" look over her shoulder. Raven's lips twitched, mostly because the look was lost on Matthew—exactly what the little girl had planned. Raven had a feeling she'd have to stay on her toes now that Jamie knew Matthew wouldn't put up with her being sassy. All the digs from the kid would come on the sly and for the purpose of challenging Raven to tattle. Raven almost looked forward to the challenge.

She fell into step beside the two. "What's your favorite baseball team?"

"What's yours?"

"Royals."

Jamie gave a disgusted snort and pointed to her ball cap. A telltale red bird was embroidered on the bill. "I'm a Cards fan. The Royals stink."

Indignation spread through Raven, but she held her cool. What did an eight-year-old know about a team making a comeback someday anyhow?

Matthew laughed, obviously sensing her bristle. "Hey, even you have to admit the Cardinals have given Missouri a little more to brag about in the past few years than the Royals."

Raven sniffed and shrugged. "They're building the team back up. Just wait. This season they'll go all the way. Who knows, maybe we'll watch the Cardinals and the Royals face off in the Series."

Jamie stopped, bringing Matthew to an abrupt halt as well. Raven took a step beyond then turned around. "What's wrong?"

"Dad and me always watch baseball together." She emphasized her words with a pointed stare. "Alone."

Raven's cheeks warmed as she realized that she'd implied she'd still be around in a few months. She glanced at Matthew, who met her gaze with guarded eyes. Drawing a deep breath, she turned back to Jamie and grinned. "Look, kid, what are the chances the Royals are really going to make it to the playoffs, let alone win the championship?"

Suspicion clouded Jamie's eyes, but she nodded. "Well, just so you know…*we* always watch baseball—just us."

"And I wouldn't dream of interfering with your time alone with your dad."

Awkward silence surrounded the three as they made their way down the street trying to find a ride where the line wasn't so long they'd have to wait an hour for a two-minute thrill. When they passed a rest-room building, Jamie shook free of Matt's hand and headed toward the side marked Ladies. "I have to go."

Matt cut a quick glance to Raven.

Raven nodded. "I'll go with her."

She trailed the little girl. Jamie noticed her walking behind and her lips twisted. "I'm not a baby."

"I know that," she said in her best matter-of-fact voice. "But you're not the only one who drank too much this morning."

"Oh."

"Okay, Jamie. Let's make a deal about the whole bathroom thing."

"Like what?"

"When you get done, wait inside the stall until I say you can come out, okay?"

"Why?"

"Because, as you pointed out earlier, children shouldn't run around the park alone and even bathrooms aren't safe. *Capisce?*"

The little girl hesitated, stubbornness oozing from every square inch of her.

Raven gathered a steadying breath. "Look, do it for your dad. He'll worry about you every time you go to the bathroom if you don't promise."

She gave a sigh. "Okay."

Raven watched her walk into a stall. She was forced to wait a minute before another one became available.

When she opened the door and walked out, she washed her hands and called, "All right, Jamie. You can come on out." The little girl didn't answer, so Raven stepped to the stall where Jamie had entered, and knocked.

"Occupied," came a woman's voice on the other side of the door. Raven's heart lurched. "Jamie?"

No one answered. "Jamie!" The stall opened and a fifty-something woman stepped out, indignation lining her face.

"I'm sorry, ma'am. Did you see a little girl come out of there? She was supposed to wait for me."

The woman's expression instantly took on a look of understanding and even a hint of concern. "No. It was empty when I came in."

Panic seized Raven and she raced outside, dread of telling Matthew she'd lost his daughter mingling with every image of terror her imagination could conjure up.

She scanned the street. Matthew stood alone, hand stuffed in his pockets. "Matthew," she called. "Have you seen Jamie?"

He frowned and closed the distance between them. "I just got back out here. There was a line on the men's side. What do you mean?"

"Jamie's not in the bathroom. I told her to stay in the stall until I said she could come out."

Horror widened Matthew's eyes. He gripped her arm, fingers of pain licking her soft flesh. "Are you sure?"

Tears stung her eyes. "I looked everywhere. She's gone."

Matthew released her arm and whipped around. "Jamie!"

* * *

"Okay, where's my dad?"

He glanced down at the little girl. Her lips were pursed in disdain and her hands planted firmly on slim hips. Resentment welled inside him and he had to fight to keep from slapping her into the cotton-candy vendor. He hated kids. Especially smart-mouthed little girls who were too savvy for their own good. He looked down at her through mirrored sunglasses and forced a smile. "Remember, he said to buy you the cotton candy and wait for him here."

She gave him a suspicious sneer. "How do I know you're not lying?"

Mindful of the adults nearby, and the need to keep the kid's voice down, he bent over, resting his palms on his knees until he was eye-level with the little brat. It took every bit of control to keep a conciliatory tone. "Look, I'm a guard at this park. Would they hire a guard who couldn't be trusted? Besides, if your dad hadn't told me to keep an eye on you, how would I know your name is Jamie?" Besides the fact that he'd heard Strong call after the kid. That had been a stroke of luck.

She squinted, as though considering his words. He'd resorted to the "Your daddy said for you to come with me" line used by so many predators, not sure she'd go alone with him. As smart as this kid seemed to be, she'd bought the lie. That was a chilling thought. "Okay. I want purple cotton candy. That's what Dad always gets me."

Glancing over his shoulder, he touched her back to move her forward toward the vendor. It wouldn't take Strong more than a few minutes to remember the girl had asked for cotton candy earlier and locate the nearest one, looking for the precocious kid. Especially with a reporter helping him out.

"Jamie!" His heart rate doubled as he heard the call.

"That's my dad! Over here!" She turned and craned her neck to see around the adults blocking her path.

Ahh, goal accomplished.

He smiled and slipped from the line. Melting into the crowd, he pulled off his hat and wig and tossed the disguise into the nearest garbage can.

Now they would know he was serious.

He was watching....

Chapter Ten

Matthew carried his sleeping daughter inside the house and up the stairs—thanking God that he still had her to hold close after today's near-kidnapping. Images of what might have happened sent shards of fear into his heart.

Jamie adjusted herself in his arms. Her soft sigh tickled his neck. Instinctively, Matt pulled her warm body closer. He couldn't hold her tight enough. When he reached her room, he pulled back the covers and reluctantly lowered her to the bed. He didn't want to let her go. Needed to feel her against his heart. With a sigh, he adjusted the comforter around her shoulders and stood back.

Tears stung his eyes as he watched her beautiful, sleeping form. Such a tiny creature, full of fun and life. And more spunk than any two little girls had any business possessing, let alone one—especially at eight years old.

How could she have been duped into walking away with a complete stranger? Hadn't he drilled all the dangers into her head since she was a toddler? If only she had been able to give a detailed description of the guy, maybe they'd have some sort of chance to find him. But by the time the police had questioned Jamie, she was too shaken herself to be of much help and had merely described the man as having red hair and wearing shiny—which Matt had taken to mean mirrored—sunglasses. And he was dressed as a park guard. Otherwise there was no way Jamie would have gone with him. He'd drilled safety rules into her head too many times. All the police could do was take a statement. The park issued an alert, and P.D. manpower devoted some time to searching. But nothing had turned up. The man was most likely wearing a stolen uniform and a possibly a wig. They'd never find him now.

Matt walked to the windows and checked the locks, pulled the shades, then with one more glance toward his daughter, he stepped into the hallway.

"Matt, honey, I thought I heard you come in."

Matthew turned to find his mother gliding toward him, her steps a mix of the grace and confidence that encompassed her personality and made her so popular with men and women alike. He bent and kissed her smooth cheek. "Jamie fell asleep on the way here. I just put her to bed."

She patted his shoulder. "You're home earlier than I expected you would be. Have you eaten supper?"

He shook his head. "I'm not hungry. Jamie may wake up hungry later, though. None of us ate much today."

"Anything wrong?"

Hesitating only a moment, Matthew nodded. "Come into my office so we can talk." There was no point in trying to spare her the details. As soon as Jamie woke up, everyone in the household would know about her ordeal—which had only become an "ordeal" for the little girl after she'd realized that Matthew hadn't, nor would he ever, instruct anyone she didn't know to take her to get cotton candy or anything else.

His mother's face drained of color as he relayed the details. "Oh, my." She lifted a trembling hand to her throat. "We need tighter security. How could Raven have allowed that child out of her sight?"

"Don't blame Raven, Mother. She took every precaution. She doesn't know our Jamie like we do." He gave her a lopsided smile. "What would you have done?"

His mother scowled, but nodded in concession. "I suppose you're right. Honestly, something needs to be done about that girl's disobedience."

"I've wrestled with whether or not to punish her for disobeying Raven, but I didn't have the heart. Once she realized what might have happened, she was pretty subdued the rest of the day."

"Little wonder." She heaved a sigh. "Do you think she should stop playing baseball this summer?"

"I couldn't take that away from her. I'll just have to be careful never to be late picking her up from practice."

"Yes." A frown made a V between her eyebrows. "Do you have any idea who might have taken her, or do you think it was random?"

Matthew shook his head. "I wish I knew. I suspected Ray."

"Ray?" A gasp escaped her lips. "Do you really think he might?"

He scrubbed at his chin and expelled a frustrated sigh. "I think he'd do anything for a buck. Even try to use his daughter against us."

"Your daughter," his mother said firmly. "She will never be his."

Affection surged through Matthew. He smiled. "I know that. But he could try to use her against us for profit."

"We'll never allow it. I'm calling the police." She

rose from her chair and reached for the phone on Matthew's desk.

"Wait, Mom. Don't. The St. Louis police have already got all this on file. We'll be more careful with Jamie from now on."

She dropped back into her chair, her face awash in color. "Do you really think it might have been Ray?"

"I don't know. James described him with the same hair as Aunt Casey."

"Red, huh? Well, that rules out Ray." She sucked in her cheek and held it there with her teeth—the only nervous habit Matt had ever observed in his mother. "Unless he was wearing a wig."

Matt gave a somber nod. "I know. Don't worry. I'll make sure no one ever has the opportunity to take her again."

"Dad?" Jamie's sleepy voice halted their conversation. Matthew glanced up to find his daughter standing in the doorway.

"What are you doing out of bed, sport?" He rolled his chair away from his desk and patted his lap. Jamie came to him willingly. He pulled her close, breathing in the soft scent of baby shampoo.

"I'm scared," she whispered. "I dreamed a man took me away from you and Grams and Aunt Casey."

"Well, don't you worry your sweet head about that." Matthew's mother moved around the desk and caressed the child's hair. "Your daddy and I are going to make sure nothing like what happened today ever happens again. Now. Are you hungry? Your daddy said you barely ate anything today."

Jamie nodded. "Can I have chicken fingers?"

Matthew hid a grin against the top of Jamie's head. His mother was appalled at the very sight of processed food in her freezer, but Matthew insisted they keep it around for the times when they needed quick calories on a busy day. Jamie instinctively knew her grandmother would deny her nothing after what had happened today, especially after what *might* have happened.

Predictably, his mother gave a loving smile and held out her hand. "Chicken fingers it is, my sweet," she said.

Matthew watched them leave, his heart nearly splitting in two with love, worry, relief. Becoming a parent had been the most incredible experience of his life and the most terrifying. And never more so than this moment. The thought of losing his little girl was intolerable and he wouldn't allow it.

His thoughts shifted to Raven. She'd barely spoken a word during the rest of the day, except to encourage him not to pull up stakes and head home immediately after the incident.

"Matt," she'd said, "Jamie feels badly enough. Don't take the park away from her. The guy's long gone. And if he'd wanted to kidnap Jamie, she'd be long gone too. Deal with this later. "

It was a crazy idea. He'd wanted to snatch Jamie up and take her home, lock her in a tower like the princess she was, and keep her safe forever. The last thing he wanted to do was expose her to thousands of strangers, hundreds of miles from home. But the remorse in his daughter's eyes had melted his heart. They'd stayed, gone on rides, pretended to have a great time. But all day, he'd sensed watchful eyes upon them. He wasn't sure if the creeped-out feeling came from the power of suggestion, or if his instincts were actually working for him. Either way, he'd made sure Jamie didn't leave his sight except for the most necessary moments, in which case, Raven stood watch with the tenacity of a guard outside Buckingham Palace.

On impulse, he grabbed the phone and dialed Raven's number. The machine picked up on the second ring. A grimace tightened his lips. He definitely was not in the mood to talk to technology. With a sigh, he dropped the receiver back into its cradle.

He tapped his computer keyboard to clear the screen saver, then downloaded his e-mail. He noticed it immediately. A user name he'd never seen in his box. Nothing in the subject line. His heart thundered in his ears as he double-clicked and a new box appeared on his screen.

How did Jamie enjoy the cotton candy? Do you understand now how serious I am?

Matt sat back and read and reread the e-mail. *Lord, what does this guy want?* He wasn't asking for anything. Just making cryptic threats. If he asked for money and signed his name, Matthew could take this to the police, but without anything to go on, they'd never believe it was Ray.

The phone rang.

Raven. His heart gave a lurch.

"Hi," she said, sounding a little breathless. Nerves? Or exertion? "I saw your name on caller ID. You should block your name, you know. Anyone can get your number."

A jolt shot through him at her words. "Raven, how would someone get another person's e-mail address?"

"Who are you looking for?"

"No one. But I got an e-mail just now from the guy at Adventure Park today."

"What? Are you kidding me?"

"I wish I were. When I tried to e-mail back, my server showed no record of that address."

"Forward me the e-mail, I can find him."

"How?"

"There are all kinds of e-mail-tracking methods and software. And if all else fails I'll call a contact at the Kansas City P.D. We'll find this bozo and get him off your back."

Relief swept through him, a sense that everything was going to be okay. "Thank you, Raven. I'm glad you're around through all of this."

A pregnant pause bloated the air between them until an intake of breath signaled her intention to speak. "I'm glad I am, too. Jamie is…"

He chuckled. "A brat?"

"I was going to say 'a real keeper.' You two are lucky to have each other."

"She needs a mother." The words left his mouth before he thought.

"Yeah, so do I." Her snappy comeback flashed an image across Matt's mind—Raven receiving the news of her mother's death. The cry of despair, the phone crashing to the floor. She'd dropped to her knees, holding her head between her arms. Guttural moans had wrenched from her body. Animalistic, and yet grief that only the human soul could express. Matthew had never before or since observed such explosive emotional pain.

"Hey, you still here?" Raven's voice cut into the image, drawing Matt from the horror of that day, the heartbreak of a couple of weeks later, when he'd watched her walk away.

"I'm here."

"I'm sorry for making it about me. Of course a little girl needs a mom. But don't sell yourself short. You've done a great job with Jamie."

"I'm afraid I've treated her too much like a son. She's such a tomboy."

"She'd have probably been a tomboy anyway. If you had tried to dress her in pink and ribbons she'd have probably fought you tooth and nail. Look at my sister Keri. She could fish, play ball and climb trees with the best of them. Still can—which comes in handy with twin boys to raise. As a matter of fact, I imagine she could take most men in a one-on-one fight if she had to. And she still managed to snag her Prince Charming."

"Okay, you've made your case. I feel better." He smiled into the empty room.

"Good. Glad to hear it. Okay, I am looking at the e-mail you forwarded. This guy is really spooky, isn't he?"

"Very."

"Listen, any chance this is a personal thing? I mean not just some crazy stalker, but someone with a real reason to threaten your family? Personal vendetta stuff? What about Jamie's biological father?"

Raven was too good. No sense keeping Ray's extortion from her. Especially if she could help. "I don't know. It's possible. But I don't want to go into it over the phone."

If nothing else, today's incident followed by this e-mail message had convinced him that he was not as secure as he'd once believed.

"Gotcha. How about meeting for breakfast tomorrow? We can go over everything and decide how to go about finding this creep."

"Breakfast won't work. We have church in the morning."

"Oh, yeah." Church.

Raven grimaced at the flatness of her own tone. The only times she'd stepped inside a church during the years since her mother's funeral were for Keri's and then Denni's weddings. But of course, Matt would still attend.

"Okay, then…"

"Why don't you join us and then come over to the house for Sunday dinner?"

Warning! Warning! Red lights and sirens strobed through her. "Uh, that's a little too much like…"

"Me taking you home to meet the folks?" Matt chuckled.

"Sort of."

"How about throwing caution to the wind and doing it anyway? I promise to inform the family that it's a strategy lunch and they are not to read any white lace and promises into it."

"Oh sure, just like you promised to tell Jamie I was nothing more than an old college chum?"

"Are you doubting my integrity?" His feigned offense brought a quick smile to Raven's lips.

"Highly questioning it, as a matter of fact."

"Look, what does it matter what conclusions they draw? I want you here. For any reason. Will you come?"

Raven hugged her knees to her chest. She squeezed her eyes shut. "Okay," she breathed out before her refusal could form on her lips.

"Okay? Just like that? Are you sure?"

Recovering a bit of composure, Raven nodded. So maybe no one else was in the room, but the physical confirmation bolstered her courage. "Yes, I'm sure."

"I'm glad. I'll be there at ten o'clock to pick you up for church. Oh, hey, I have to go. Jamie's back in here and I need to tuck her into bed. I'll see you tomorrow."

Panic seized Raven. "Matt, wait!"

Too late. The line went dead.

Her throat tightened and her pulse quickened with the beginnings of what could only be an anxiety attack.

She'd only agreed to lunch at the Strong mansion. Never, ever, in million years had she planned to go to church. Raven glanced at the clock, debating whether to call Matt back and set him straight. But no. He was busy with Jamie.

Gathering a deep breath, she squared her shoulders and resigned herself to a pew-sitting, hymn-singing, head-bowing church service.

After all, what harm could one service do?

Chapter Eleven

Drat! Parking oneself on a pew after fifteen years of no church attendance was like coming home after living in a non-English-speaking country for decades. Raven barely understood the language anymore. Churchese.

She sat stock-still, unsure what was appropriate, and unwilling to make a spectacle of herself by doing the wrong thing—especially if someone recognized her from the news broadcasts.

Seated next to Mrs. Strong, Raven felt as though she might as well have been Fergie sitting next to the Queen Mum, for all the warmth she received. Most horrifying was that, try as she might to stay stiff and unmoved, inexplicable tears burned just behind her eyes when the congregation began to sing "'Tis So Sweet to Trust in Jesus."

Egads! Tears trickled down her face, first one, then another and another until there was no dignified way to hide the fact that she was crying. She sniffled. Mrs. Strong pressed a tissue into her hand.

Nodding her thanks, Raven kept her tear-blurred gaze

averted to the hymnal on her lap. Mercifully, the preacher took his place at the pulpit next and she was able to regain and maintain composure throughout the rest of the service. When the service closed, she excused herself to the restroom where she wiped away smudges of mascara. Dread tugged at her heart. How would she explain this to Matthew? Especially when she didn't understand, herself.

Matthew stood waiting in the foyer when she emerged. A tender smile touched his lips. "Ready?"

"Where's Jamie?"

"Mother picked her up from Kids' Church. She'll drive her home."

He opened the church door and allowed her to precede him outside. The air smoldered in the summer breeze.

"Whew," Matthew said, loosening his tie. "Leaving the air conditioning to come out in this is a shocker."

"No kidding. Tony, our chief meteorologist, says we're in for another week of this heat without much chance of rain."

"Well, it's his job to know, isn't it?"

"Yep, and our Tony is the number-one weather guy in Kansas City."

The small talk helped Raven's taut nerves begin to relax as they drove out of the parking lot and into the traffic. The farther away from the church they drove, the better she felt.

To her relief, no mention was made of her meltdown during the service.

"So, how was Jamie this morning?"

"Not great. She had trouble sleeping last night— nightmares."

"I'm so sorry."

He pounded the steering wheel. "I've got to find this guy and get him out of our life. I hate the feeling that he's a real threat to Jamie."

"What about going to the police?"

"We did that in St. Louis."

"I know, but that was over what happened yesterday. You have more now. Maybe you should show them the e-mail, let them do a trace."

"Could they do anything you can't do?"

"Well, no. Not until he's actually caught."

"Then let's not take a chance the press will get wind of this. Jamie doesn't need to see reminders on the news. She's shaken enough as it is."

Raven knew he hadn't considered her employment status when he'd made the "press" remark. Rather than being insulted, she enjoyed the idea that he trusted her. Apparently it hadn't crossed his mind that she might report this incident with Jamie as news. And amazingly, she hadn't even considered it.

A definite sign of character growth.

"Here we are," Matthew announced.

She drew a delighted breath at the sight of Matthew's home as they drew up before it. "I'd forgotten how beautiful this house is."

Matthew smiled. "Thank you."

"You were one lucky kid growing up in a place like this, Matt. You must have had a lot of friends inviting themselves over."

"Well, only from kids whose parents were in Dad's political party." He laughed. "Just kidding."

"Is Jamie going to your fancy old alma mater?"

"Mother wouldn't have it any other way," he drawled. "To tell you the truth, I'd love to take Jamie and raise her in a normal house in the suburbs somewhere. Away from so-called upper-class society. Mother's a wonderful woman, but she has her notions."

"That's an intriguing idea. I think Jamie would love to live in a neighborhood with other kids to hang out with."

"Intriguing, but not practical, I'm afraid. Especially now that we've become some sort of target."

Raven reached across the seat and touched his shoulder. "We'll get to the bottom of this. I promise."

He covered her hand with his. "I'm glad you've come back into my life, Raven. For whatever reason. It helps having someone to talk to about this."

"What do you mean, 'for whatever reason'?"

Matt released a heavy sigh. "Kellie told me about your race for anchor."

Her pulse quickened. Raven frowned. "Kellie Cruise?" The interloper, climber, daughter of the station manager? How on earth… Oh, yeah…

"My parents know hers. Mother is great friends with Kellie's mother. She was just a kid last time I saw her until I ran into her the other night…coincidentally, the same place I first ran into you."

Ignoring the innuendo, she worked at wrapping her mind around the reminder that Kellie had the same edge as she had for Matt's story. "At the gym?" The little sneak.

"Yep. At the gym."

Unable to bear the questioning look in his eyes, she averted her gaze, cleared her throat. He laced his fingers with hers. "I have a pretty good idea that you didn't walk into Randy's that night by mistake."

A feather-soft kiss warmed her fingers, drawing her gaze upward to his. She couldn't speak. Couldn't admit that she'd callously looked him up in effort to use the love they'd shared for her personal gain. But awareness shone in his eyes and she knew she didn't have to confess. He chuckled.

"You never could tell a lie, Raven. You have guilt written all over that pretty face."

"Matt...I..."

"Don't..." He pressed a finger to her lips, and allowed it to linger, as warm and gentle as a kiss. "If that was your motive for looking me up, I can live with it. It doesn't say much for my manly charms, and that's a little ego-bruising. But, as I said, I can live with it."

Raven opened her mouth against his finger. "Wait," he said gently, applying more pressure. "Let me finish." He slid his hand upward to cup her cheek.

She nodded, fighting the urge to lean into his palm.

"I want to pursue the feelings I'm having for you. But I need you to know I will not put Jamie on display for anyone. Not even you. So you have to make a choice. If you want a place—your rightful place, I might add—in my life, it'll mean giving up the story you're looking for."

Raven closed her eyes, envisioning her career going round and round in circles until finally flushing down the bowl of life.

The balance scales in her mind weighed her options.

She cared about him...she really did. But what if they didn't work out again? Where would she be? Stuck in a low-position job, reporting to Kellie—the cheerleader—Cruise. She swallowed hard. "Matt..."

A scowl twisted his lips. He dropped his hand from her face. "I guess that's my answer."

"Wait a minute. No it isn't." She grabbed his arm. "You have to understand...you're asking me to give up something I've wanted for a long time on the off chance that you and I are going to work out."

"Why shouldn't we?"

"Well, look at last time." She grimaced, wishing she hadn't brought that up.

Predictably, Matt jumped on it. "Yeah, let's do look at last time. You walked away without an explanation. Our relationship seems to rest firmly in your hands once again. Are we going to write a new story? Or is history about to repeat itself?"

Raven drew in her bottom lip. If the scales tipped on the side of work, she already had a thrilling enough story as it was, and something the St. Louis police could corroborate. All she'd have to do was report it, standing just outside the gate of the mansion. Ask rhetorical questions such as… "One has to wonder, is Mr. Strong's fear for his family's safety what compelled him to pull out of the race?" She wouldn't even have to bring up the girl's biological father extorting money. This kidnapping threat would be enough to win her points at the station. She'd have to act quickly, though. Matthew would be old news before long. Inwardly, she groaned. So much for that newfound character growth.

"You've got to be kidding me." Anger flashed in Matt's eyes, and rang in his voice. He slid closer and pulled her tightly into his arms. "Are you really going to walk away from us again?"

Tremors of longing surged through her stomach, igniting long-suppressed feelings. "Matthew," she murmured.

He pressed his forehead to hers. "Don't tell me your heart isn't racing as much as mine."

"You know it is."

"Then how can there even be a moment's pause in your mind?"

"How can you ask me to choose? Do you know how long I've waited for a chance at anchor? I deserve it."

"You do deserve it. But at what risk? My daughter's safety?"

"I would never give out Jamie's name. I'd just mention that you might have pulled out of the race in an effort to protect your family."

"Raven…"

Her phone chirped, saving her any need to answer. "Hello?"

"Where are you?" Ken's voice on the other end of the line forced a frown between Raven's eyes.

"I'm with a friend. What's up?"

"I just thought I'd tell you there's been a fight down at one of the inner-city missions. Someone got shot in the crossfire. I got an inside tip from Lucas at the Kansas City P.D. It's our story first if you can meet me over there."

Alarm shot through Raven. "Which mission, Ken?"

"Victory Mission."

Raven's throat went dry. "I have to go," she croaked.

"Okay, meet you in a few minutes."

Without a good-bye, she disconnected the call and speed-dialed Keri's cell. Her voice mail picked up. With a growl, Raven looked up the number for the mission in her contacts list. Ten rings later, she finally gave up.

"Something wrong?" Matthew asked.

"I'm not sure. Can you take me down to the Victory Mission?"

"What is it? You're white as a sheet."

"There was a shooting down there." She gave him the address.

"Inner city?"

She nodded. "Would you rather I take a cab?"

"Of course not. What happened?"

"A fight broke out and someone was shot. That's all I know. My little sister, Keri, and her husband run the place."

"Let me see your phone," he instructed, restarting the car.

She handed it over and he punched in a number. "Mother? Raven and I aren't going to make it to dinner after all. You and Casey and Jamie eat without us."

Pause.

"I'll explain later." He disconnected the call and returned her phone.

"Thank you, Matt."

Raven watched him maneuver through traffic. Confident, determined to get her where she needed to be.

As if sensing her perusal, he turned his head, capturing her gaze. He gave her a reassuring smile and took her hand. "I'm praying your sister and brother-in-law are safe. But I'll be right there with you just in case…"

"I appreciate it."

He diverted his attention back to the traffic. Raven leaned her head against the seat. It was so nice to let someone else take charge for a change. Though she typically fought against that instinctual male protectiveness and TLC, she had to admit that for this moment, having Matt taking care of her gave her a wrapped-in-a-warm-quilt-on-a-cold-night feeling. She'd never been crazy about Keri working at the mission. Besides the obvious danger, the thought of her kid sister giving up a promising career in law enforcement—the opportunity to be the first female, not to mention the youngest, chief of police in Briarwood, Missouri, their hometown—grated on Raven. But there was something undeniable about the love Keri and Justin shared.

Raven knew her sister couldn't resist following her heart—something Raven had never had the gumption to do.

ROMANCE title

Raven knew her way around. She'd even followed her boss back in with her camera that never left the sidewalk.

Chapter Twelve

The wail of a siren sliced through the stifling air as an ambulance whizzed past Matthew's car, heading in the opposite direction. Raven's heart nearly thundered from her chest. The uncertainty of knowing what she'd find in a few minutes taunted her with images of the outcome she dreaded most. Losing another member of her family.

They drove another block before red and blue lights came into view from the two police cars parked outside the mission.

Matthew scanned the street. "There's not going to be any place to park, Raven."

"Let me out, then," she said, more sharply than she'd intended. "I have to get to my sister."

"Honey, I know you're worried, but I can't drop you off in the middle of that crowd." He motioned toward a gathering of onlookers three and four people deep across the sidewalk.

Ken's grizzled form appeared through the gathering. He spotted her instantly. With one arm cradling his camera, he waved frantically with the other, then motioned for her to hurry.

"Look, Matt. There's Ken, my camera guy. I'll be safe. Let me out. You can go around to the alley behind the mission. There's a four-car garage back there for Keri's and Justin's cars. They added the other two for situations like this." She grabbed a pen from her purse. "Here, give me your hand." She scribbled some numbers on his palm.

He kept his gaze on the thickening traffic. "What did you write?

"The combination to the garage lock so you can park your car. It's digital."

"I think you should just wait and let me walk in with you."

"That'll take too long, Matt. Just stop and let me out."

Like it or not, Matt was forced by the traffic in front of him to brake. Without bothering to wait for the car to come to a full stop, Raven jumped out. She dashed in and out of the dozens of people milling about on the sidewalk all the way up to the mission.

Any other day she might have been concerned about walking alone on this street, even with Ken standing fifty feet from her, but now her only thought was for her sister.

He elbowed his way through the crowd and met her halfway. "Took you long enough," he wheezed, gulping for breath.

"Sheesh, Ken, if you don't stop smoking you're going to lose a lung."

"Don't nag."

"Fine. I don't have time to argue with you."

She brushed by him, heading toward the doors.

He easily fell into step beside her. "Hey, they're not going to let you in. Let's do the lead-in now and find a few people in the crowd who might have seen something."

"I'm not here for a story," she said over her shoulder, pulling on the door. "It's locked."

"Come again?" Ken grasped her arm and pulled her back. "Do you think they're actually going to let you inside? The cops have it locked down. This is a crime scene."

"My sister and her husband run this place," she said simply.

"Hot dog! Then let's get in there and get our story." He planted a fat kiss on her cheek. "You're the best."

"Ken! I don't know if my baby sister was in that ambulance or not! I couldn't care less about this stupid story at the moment. If it's so important to you, call Kellie and see if she'll come down here."

She shook him off and shoved her way to the door again. Cupping her hands around her eyes to suppress her peripheral vision, she peered through the window. Relief weakened her knees at the sight of Keri, sitting on a bench against the far wall. She cuddled an African-American toddler against her chest, her chin resting on the child's head.

Raven slapped on the glass, "Keri! Let me in. It's Raven." Keri didn't look up, but one of a handful of officers spied her and jerked his thumb, a signal for her to beat it. She scowled and pointed toward Keri.

He turned toward Keri. She looked up and her ashen face brightened. She nodded to the officer. He opened the door.

Raven slipped inside and headed for her sister, who hadn't budged from her place by the wall.

Ken's voice coming from the door stopped her forward trek. "Rave, tell this guy I'm with you." She turned to find the officer bodily keeping Ken from entering the mission.

"He's telling the truth, officer."

Raven turned her attention back to Keri. "I'm so relieved to see you're okay. Where's Justin?"

"In the ambulance," Keri said, her voice barely above a whisper.

Alarm shot through Raven. "Kere! Why aren't you with him? Is he okay?"

"I had to stay with Anaya."

"Give her to me. I'll watch her. Do you want Matt to drive you to the hospital?"

She shook her head. "Justin can handle things without me."

Raven frowned. Clearly Keri was in shock. "Did the paramedics check you over?"

Confusion crossed her features. "Me? Why would they?"

"I don't know, but you seem pretty unemotional for someone whose husband was just shot."

"Shot?" She rolled her eyes. "Good grief, Rave, Justin wasn't shot."

"Then why is he riding in the ambulance?"

"To stay with Anaya's mother. She caught a bullet trying to get Anaya out of the way."

Raven released a heavy breath. "I'm so relieved it wasn't Justin."

She caressed the sleeping toddler's head. Tears formed in her eyes. "Raven, they said Mary probably won't make it. What is poor Anaya going to do?"

"What about her dad?"

"Mary and Anaya have been living here since we opened the women's section of the shelter. Mary was a prostitute. She doesn't know who Anaya's father is."

"Have you gotten in touch with Social Services yet?"

Keri pulled the sleeping child closer and shook her

head. "Not until I have to." She glanced up and Raven met her teary gaze. "Mary was this close to contacting her family. But she never told me anything about them other than that they don't live in Kansas City."

Raven felt the weight of the loaded statement. "A child with a family who might want her, but no way to find them. That stinks."

"Yes, it does. This whole thing stinks. I'm just glad the shooter is in jail." She shook her head. "Too bad that's not going to bring Mary back."

Raven sat beside her sister and slipped her arm around Keri's shoulders, pulling her close. "I'm sorry, Keri. Is there anything I can do?"

"I'm just glad you're here. How'd you know anyway?"

"Ken called me."

"Your camera guy? But…how…? Did he know you and I are sisters?"

"No, he was looking for a scoop."

Keri sat up straight and turned steady, scrutinizing eyes on her.

Raven's defenses rose. "Hey, don't look at me like that. I promise I didn't come down here for a story."

"Then what's the camera for?" She nodded toward Ken, who was talking to the officer who'd tried to keep him out.

Waving, Raven dismissed the question. "That camera is Ken's security blanket. He wouldn't leave it behind any more than he'd leave his cigarettes."

"Do you want a story, Rave? I've been seeing that Kellie on air lately. I thought you'd be a sure replacement for Bruce King."

"Well, technically, he's not retired yet, but he had a mild heart attack and he won't be returning to work. Kellie has anchored a couple of times." The little sneak.

She always made sure she was in the right place at the right time.

Keri signaled for one of the officers. "How much of this is hush-hush for now? My sister is from Channel 23. Can she do a news report on this?"

"Since we already have the shooter in custody, thanks to you, Mrs. Kramer, I don't see why she shouldn't do the story."

"Great," Raven interjected, though the young officer was staring at Keri with more than a little admiration. "Thanks, officer. We won't keep you from your investigation."

Reluctantly, he moved away.

"I can't believe it! That guy was hanging all over you. Doesn't he know you're married?"

Keri sent her a dubious grin. "He wasn't hitting on me."

"Then I'd like to know what that was."

"I got the gun away from the shooter, that's all. Now, Junior over there thinks I'm neat-o."

Laughter bubbled to Raven's lips.

"I hate to break up this touching sister moment," Ken said in normal Ken fashion—cut to the chase, get the job done, hurry back to the station and clock out so he could throw back half a dozen beers before going home to his lonely little apartment. Even if he had to be rude to get it done.

Raven frowned, but couldn't say much in this instance. He was right.

"This isn't the sort of story that's going to get me an anchor job, but it is newsworthy."

"A woman was shot and will more than likely die." Keri's fierce voice raised Raven's brow. "Maybe it's not that big a story to you, but to her orphaned child it's pretty significant."

"Take it easy, Kere. I wasn't implying it's not heart-wrenching. But the world is used to these random acts of violence. An ex-prostitute getting caught in a cross-fire isn't that big a deal to most people, whether she dies or not. I'm sorry if that upsets you, hon. But that's the way things are."

"I don't think you give people enough credit. How could they not care? Look what happened to Mahoney House after you did a report on it. When people found out Denni was trying to help former foster-care girls adjust to adulthood and keep them from following a pattern of welfare and out-of-wedlock babies, they started writing and sending money. She had enough donations to meet her budget for a year."

Raven stared at her sister and tried not to give expression to the smug amusement playing inside her chest. Keri thought with her heart. So did Denni. Raven needed to be more practical. That was the difference between her and her two sisters. Another difference.

Perhaps the cut-to-the-chase part of her came from her father. A sudden surge of desire nearly overwhelmed her. To connect with Sonny and her biological father as soon as possible.

"I'll tell you what," she said. "How about if I film the little girl and tell her story in the report?"

Hope gleamed in Keri's eyes. "Would you?"

Raven nodded. "I can't guarantee it won't be cut during editing, but I'll do my best."

"Thank you, Rave."

"Okay, Ken. Let's do a lead-in and get this to the station."

Matthew's pulse quickened as Raven's form appeared on the twenty-seven-inch TV screen. He grabbed the remote and pressed Record. She was wasted on a local cable channel. Raven shone brightly as a reporter. But as far as he was concerned, she should be working for a real network—reaching her full potential. His father's time in Washington had yielded contacts who might take a look at her tape.

He lay stretched out on his bed and watched. She was back at the mission, giving a live report to go with her tape. She stood in the street with the mission front as a backdrop.

"Mary Ford died en route to the hospital this afternoon. She leaves behind a beautiful two-year-old daughter named Anaya." The station cut to the tape Ken and Raven had recorded earlier. Keri held the little girl in her arms. "We're asking for anyone who might have information about Mary's family to come forward."

"What will happen to Anaya for now?" Kellie asked.

Raven nodded. "The directors of Victory Mission are emergency foster parents. They can keep her for a little while. But if her family isn't found, she will eventually be placed in a permanent foster home."

Anaya's face filled the screen once more, her rosy lips slightly open as she slept against Keri's chest. Raven's voice dubbed over. "This little girl has a family somewhere. A family who might want her. Her mother may have started off in life with a few bumps in her road, but she had turned things around and was days away from contacting them to make amends. There are too many children without families. Perhaps as a community we can make a difference in the life of one beautiful little girl named Anaya."

The screen split to show a photograph of the mother on one side and the child on the other, then switched back to Raven. The crowded street behind her was still cluttered with onlookers trying to capture three-and-a-half seconds of air time. Movement in the corner of the screen caught Matthew's attention. Cold recognition blasted him like a freezing wind, and he sat bolt upright.

"Ray!"

Anger burned in his chest, melting the shock and spurring him to action. If Ray was hanging out around the mission, it wouldn't take much for Matthew to find him. He was going to pay dearly for the note, e-mail, and Jamie's near-kidnapping.

Chapter Thirteen

At ten o'clock the next morning, Keri and Justin joined Matthew in Raven's office to examine the computerized footage they'd taken the day before. Raven sat at her desk and used the mouse to pull the image in closer and adjust the size for a better view.

She turned to Keri and Justin, who stood behind her staring over her shoulder at the computer screen. "Look familiar?" she asked.

Justin frowned and shook his head. "He may have come in for meals, but I'd know him if he ever stayed in the shelter overnight." He turned to Keri. "Do you remember that guy from the meal lines?"

Peering closer, Keri scrunched her brow. "I don't think so. But I'll keep an eye out from now on."

"I appreciate it." Matthew's disappointment was more than evident. Raven's heart went out to him.

Expelling a breath, Raven sat back in the chair. She lifted her arms behind her head and laced her fingers. "There's got to be a better way to find this jerk than dumb luck."

Matt raked his fingers through his hair. "I got in

touch with his parole officer before I came over here. But she couldn't help me. Ray missed his first check-in. Probably because he knew he couldn't pass a drug test. So there's a warrant out for his arrest as it is."

"Well, so much for that." Raven unlaced her fingers and reached for Matthew's hand. "Don't worry," she said. "We'll figure out who's behind all this. If not Ray, then whoever is responsible."

Matt squeezed her hand and gave her a tender smile. "I just hope we can find him soon enough to avoid another incident." He released her and reached toward Justin. "It was nice to meet you. I appreciate your coming down here."

Justin accepted the proffered hand with a nod. "Our pleasure. I just wish we could be more help. The best I can do is offer our prayers."

"That's all anyone can do for now. And I gladly accept as much of that kind of help as I can get."

Uncomfortable, Raven averted her gaze to the floor. Just when she thought Justin might make them hold hands and say a prayer in the middle of her office, someone knocked on her door. She breathed a sigh of relief. "Come in!"

Shane Crowley, an adorable college intern with quick dimples and curly black hair, peeked in. "Sorry to interrupt."

"You're fine. What's up?"

"There's a guy out here insisting he needs to see you."

"What does he want?" She thought back over her reports during the past month. Anything controversial that might get her into trouble? Nope. Not unless one considered the exposé she'd done on the tanning-salon-owning pervert who'd installed cameras in each room.

But she doubted seriously he had the guts to confront anyone face-to-face.

Shane grinned. "Says he's your brother."

Keri laughed. "A brother, eh? That's a new way to meet you."

"This guy sort of looks like you, Raven."

Raven felt the blood drain from her face. Sonny.

"Oh, this I have to see." Keri strode toward the door.

"Wait, Kere. Let Shane deal with him." She glanced at the intern. "Tell him I can't talk now, but if he will come back later I'd be happy to sit down and find out what this is all about."

"You'll *what?*" Keri stared at her, bewilderment popping from every freckle. "Raven, you can't sit down and talk to a nut job who claims to be your *brother*."

"I agree." Matthew stepped forward. "I'll go talk to him."

"No! I think I can handle this," she said, eyeing first one then the other. "I know you only mean well, but I've had a lot of practice in dealing with fans and admirers."

Keri scowled. "Fine, have it your way. We have to go pick up the boys from swimming lessons."

"All right. I'll call you later if I hear anything about Anaya's family."

Giving her a tight squeeze, Keri whispered against her ear. "Matthew loves you still. I can tell."

Warmth crept to Raven's cheeks. "We'll see," she whispered back.

Justin wrapped her in a bear hug, his scratchy chin tickling her cheek.

"Thanks again for coming down, Justin."

"No problem. Let me know if I can do anything else."

They left and Raven turned expectantly to Matt, stubbornness plain in every line on his face. He plunked down in the nearest chair and crossed his arms over his chest.

Panic rose in Raven. Sonny was waiting. Her brother. Her secret.

"Matthew," she said slowly. "As much as I'd love to sit and talk, I'm afraid duty calls." Forcing a bright smile, she willed him to take a clue and leave.

He shook his head and set his jaw. "I'm not leaving until I know who this so-called *brother* is."

She rolled her eyes. "Why? You jealous?"

He narrowed his gaze and pushed to his feet, purpose written in each stride as he closed the distance between them. Slipping his arms around her waist, he pulled her to him in one quick movement.

Raven's heart nearly burst from her chest as his head moved closer. She could feel the warmth of his breath on her face.

"Not jealous, Raven. Just not willing to take a chance on you being harmed by someone who might not have your best interests at heart."

"H-he won't…" Her gaze lowered to his mouth. He smiled and she looked up.

"I'm going to make sure he doesn't. If I have to hold you close to me for the rest of my life, I will."

"That sounds an awful lot like a proposal," she whispered.

"It wasn't," he whispered back.

Heat seared her cheeks. She averted her gaze.

He dipped his head lower. "I proposed once. I never changed my mind. The ball is in your court. When you're ready to take the ring back, it's still yours."

His mouth closed over hers before she could process his declaration. For Raven, this wonderful kiss felt just like Christmas, landing her first job and the first morning of vacation all rolled into one. She sighed against his lips as he pulled away. "Matthew…"

"Shh, I'm not asking for you to pick up where we left off before your mother died. Just letting you know that my feelings are still the same. When and if you're ever ready to love me again, I'll be here."

Her heart shouted to her, *Admit it. Let go and let him love you!*

Before she could decide whether to accept the challenge or quiet her emotions, Matt stepped back. "Don't walk out to your car alone when you leave. Promise me."

She nodded. "I promise."

"Okay then, I'll leave you to your work. Jamie has soccer practice in an hour and I need to be there."

He dipped his head and pressed a quick kiss to her lips. "I'll call you later."

As soon as the door closed behind him, she sank into the nearest chair and buried her face in her hands.

Matthew glanced in the rearview mirror and frowned. The same blue car that had been following them since he and Jamie had pulled out of the ballpark had just reappeared through a zigzag of traffic. His heart sent up a flare to heaven. *Lord, show me where the danger is coming from. I can't protect my family if Ray keeps eluding me.*

"What's wrong, Dad?"

He glanced at his daughter. The worry clouding her eyes slashed at him. He hadn't meant to be so transparent that his daughter would worry.

"Nothing's wrong, honey."

Her face, smudged with sweat and dirt, scrunched with a dubious frown. "I can tell when you're lying to me. You keep looking in the mirror and breathing heavy."

He whipped the car out of the lane of traffic and hit the off ramp at sixty miles per hour. The blue car stayed on the freeway. Swallowing hard, Matthew returned his focus to driving.

"Okay, I mean it, Dad. What's going on? I don't recognize this street. We're not even going the right way."

Matt surveyed the street he'd pulled onto. She was right. He didn't recognize anything either. But the golden arches, standing majestically a few yards on the right, were the universal landmark. "Hey, I thought you might be hungry after all that running you did."

"Really? Can I have chicken nuggets?"

"You sure can."

"And a shake?"

"Yep."

"So nothing's wrong?"

"Everything is just fine." For now anyway.

"Okay, that's great, Ken. Thanks."

The cameraman puffed on a cigarette and nodded. "I'll wrap up here and meet you back at the station to start editing this for six o'clock."

Raven stood outside the courthouse where the serial bank robber had just been arraigned. Her afternoon had been filled with dreams of the kiss she'd shared with Matthew—until two hours ago, when she'd gotten word about the arraignment. Then rational thought fled and she'd moved on instinct. She'd dashed out to wrap up her story, calling Ken on the way. Now she felt a little lost. There would be no more robberies—at least with this guy's MO—which was a good thing, but it left her at loose ends. Barring an unexpected jailbreak, this guy wasn't news anymore until a jury of his peers found him guilty. She needed to come up with another running story.

Her thoughts turned back to Matt as she walked through the dim parking garage toward her SUV. A creepy shudder crept up her spine. Too late, she remembered that she'd promised not to walk to her car alone. She squared her shoulders and tried to squash the feeling that someone was watching her. The price of an overactive imagination.

The smell of smoke lingered in the air accompanied by heavy footsteps. She frowned. Ken?

She stopped and turned, expecting to find her cameraman behind her. Instead, a cop walked past her. That explained the footsteps, but not the cigarette smoke.

She pressed the auto unlock on her keychain and moments later left the suffocating garage. The light of day had never looked so good.

An hour after she arrived back at the station, her phone rang.

"Why'd you blow me off this morning?" A heavy, slurred voice spoke into her ear. "They treated me like I was some kind of stalker."

"I'm so sorry you felt that way, Sonny." Raven was a little tired of the way her so-called brother vented on her every time something didn't go according to his plan. "I was busy and I haven't had a chance to tell anyone about you."

"No one knows I'm alive?"

"I haven't felt comfortable sharing my news about you just yet." She smiled. "We haven't even met face-to-face. You know?"

"Well, whose fault is that?"

"Mine, I guess."

Her simple statement seemed to defuse him. "Sonny, how come our dad never calls me? Have you told him about me?"

"I want to meet you first so I can surprise him when you're ready to meet him."

"That's very sweet of you."

"He's been through enough. I just don't want him disappointed."

"What do you mean? What's he been through? Is he okay?"

"Oh, he's okay now. But my mother left us when I was about six years old." The steel in his tone brought a frown to Raven's brow. "It was hard on Dad."

"I can imagine. My mother died when I was in college."

"A dead mom isn't the same thing as being abandoned. My mother's actions were her choice."

"Of course. I'm sorry, Sonny. That must have been really hard on you and…your dad."

"Hey, *our* dad, sis." His tone lightened as quickly as it had darkened.

Sheesh, talk about bipolar.

"So, when do you want to meet? How about if I take you out tonight?"

"Dinner sounds great. I have to get this story on the six o'clock news, then I'm free for the rest of the night. Where shall we meet?"

"Do you like Italian?"

"Love it."

"There's a great little Italian joint just around the corner from your station."

"Mama Rosa's?"

"That's it."

"Okay, let's meet say…six-thirtyish?"

"I'm looking forward to it."

"Me too," Raven replied with warmth. She hung up the phone with a sense of purpose. Tonight was the night she'd finally meet her only brother.

* * *

Matthew hung up the phone and sat back in his chair. It wasn't like Raven not to answer her phone. He'd tried her work line, her home line and her cell and got voice mail on all three.

His heart lodged in his throat. What if he'd scared her off earlier with his big declaration? But she hadn't seemed scared. She'd actually seemed as moved as he had.

Still, he'd sensed she wasn't quite ready to give up the possibility of getting a story out of him. A heavy sigh escaped him. He couldn't do it. Jamie had to be protected. Could he keep his child safe and have Raven in his life too? That was the question, wasn't it?

Chapter Fourteen

Raven knew as soon as she spotted Sonny that he was her brother. His dark eyes and dark hair mirrored her own in an eerie sort of familial resemblance that she'd sort of hoped for, but hadn't really expected. He smiled and stood as she approached the table.

"Hi," she said breathlessly. "I'm not late, am I?"

He glanced at his watch and shook his head. "Right on time. Six-thirtyish, right?"

"Right."

An awkward silence fell. Neither offered to sit. Raven wasn't sure whether to hold out her hand, or move in for a quick, sisterly hug.

Sonny appeared to be having the same dilemma. He gave her a sheepish grin and bent, pressing a kiss on her cheek. Perfect.

"Shall we sit?" he asked.

Raven slid into the booth. She slipped her purse off her shoulder and settled it on the seat next to her. The waitress appeared asking for her drink order. "Diet cola," she said.

Sonny scowled. "That stuff's rat poison."

"I'll take my chances. Can't eat Italian without a diet soda."

He shrugged. "Have it your way."

Clasping her fingers in front of her, she shook her head. "I can't believe the resemblance between us. Can you?"

"Uncanny." He rimmed his water glass with his index finger. "We could be fraternal twins. But of course, I've seen you on TV so I already knew how much we look alike."

"So, tell me about yourself, Sonny. What do you do for a living?"

He stirred his straw around the ice water and met her gaze with a shrug. "This and that."

Oh, brother. That meant he was going to stick her with the check.

He laughed. "Don't worry. I have steady income. Actually, I have my Masters in Economics and I teach a couple of night classes at the University of Missouri–Kansas City. But only the Ph.D.s make enough to live on. So I also do some physical training at Fitness World."

"I see. I could use some physical training. What's your fee?" She grinned.

"Ah, well, that's where being a family member works to your advantage. I'd do it for free."

"So, are you married, Sonny?"

He shook his head. "No."

The one-word answer would have been enough to dissuade most people, but not a sister who made her living being nosy. "How come? You seem like an okay guy, and obviously you have good genes. Why hasn't some woman snagged you yet?"

"Because I haven't ever allowed myself to be snagged. Marriage is a slow form of emotional death as far as I'm concerned. My parents were proof of that. How about you? Why haven't you tied the knot yet?"

"I was engaged once."

"What happened?"

"Let's just say, my own disillusionment with life began about that time."

"You want to elaborate?"

"Not really. Suffice it to say that I decided to put my energy into building a successful career rather than giving my happiness over to a man."

The waitress appeared to take their orders, effectively cutting off Sonny's reply for a couple of minutes. When she left, he gave Raven a scrutinizing look. "Well, it seems you and I have more in common than merely sharing our biological father. We both have a jaded view of relationships."

"Seems so."

He chuckled. "Maybe we can find a therapist who gives family discounts."

Raven couldn't help but laugh with him. "Good idea."

"Do you want to see a picture of Dad?" Sonny's sudden question took her off guard and she fought to swallow down the sip of her soda without spewing it all over the table.

She swiped at her mouth with a napkin and nodded. "I'd love it." Through all of her searching, she'd never been able to locate a photo.

He pulled his wallet from the inside pocket of his tan sports coat.

Raven took the photograph with a mix of fascination and angst. She should have recognized the man staring back at her. The dark eyes, dark hair. The exotic cheekbones and full lips that had always distinguished Raven from the rest of her family. But this man was a stranger to her. Her mind conjured the familiar image of dear Mac. Daddy. The gruff cop with the gentleness of heart to cry during Hallmark commercials and Christmas programs.

"What was he like as a father?" she asked, without taking her eyes off the photo. "When you were growing up, I mean."

Sonny released a sigh that told her more than his words could have. "He wasn't the baseball playing, camping kind of dad. But I knew he loved me. He always told me it was just the two of us against the world. I guess that was his way of making me feel special."

"That was nice." Just the two of them. The words scraped Raven's heart raw.

A dubious grin quirked one side of his mouth. "Well, it was nice as long as he was between women. But Dad wasn't the kind of guy to stay celibate for long. And he couldn't just date. He was addicted to relationships."

"He never remarried?"

"No. He came close a couple of times, but it never seemed to work out."

"That's too bad. It would have been nice for you to have had a mother."

"I have a mother," he shot back. His tone once again too hard, the way she'd noted a couple of times before.

"I'm sorry. I didn't realize you stayed in contact with her."

He scowled. "I didn't. I'm sorry. I guess I do need therapy." He gave a self-deprecating smile. "A little boy abandoned by his mother and the forty-one-year-old man is still paying for it emotionally."

Instinctively, Raven reached across the table and covered his hand with hers. He snatched his back as though he'd been pricked.

Heat flamed her cheeks. "I'm sorry. I didn't mean to

cross any boundaries." But sheesh, he'd kissed her on the cheek. What was a little hand-on-hand comfort between long-lost siblings?

"No boundaries crossed." He covered his hand where hers had been. "I'm just not accustomed to being touched. It startled me."

Note to self, don't touch new brother.

"Anyway," Sonny said, nodding toward the photo Raven still held. "Feel free to keep that. I have another one."

"Thanks."

The waitress brought their meal. Raven breathed a sigh of relief and launched into small talk between bites.

"What's your favorite color?"

"Black."

Okay, that suits him.

"Where'd you go to high school?"

"Right here in Kansas City."

"What do you like to do on a cold, rainy night?"

"Read."

Now, there's common ground.

"Who is your favorite author?"

"Stephen King."

Hmm. Maybe not.

When they stood to leave, Sonny insisted on paying the bill. Raven was pleased to note he left a generous tip. They walked out of the restaurant together.

"So, Sonny," Raven said when they reached her SUV. "Now that you've met me, when do you think I can meet your dad?"

"Let me see what I can do to set that up. I'll call you, okay?"

"Sure. It's nice that you want to surprise him. I just hope he wants to meet me."

"Don't worry about that. He will."

She glanced in the rearview mirror as she drove away. He stood watching her for as long as she was able to make out his form in the dark parking lot.

A sudden shiver crawled up her spine. She had the sense that she was treading into territory rife with complications she probably wasn't ready to deal with.

Guilt plagued her at the thought of how Mac might feel if he knew she had a desire to meet her biological father. Especially since he had no idea that she'd found her original birth certificate.

Watching traffic closely, she felt around on the seat for her cell phone. She speed-dialed Mac. He answered in three rings.

"Hey Dad, how's it going?"

"What's wrong, honey? You sound upset."

How could he tell in only five words?

"Hey, can't a girl call her dad without something being wrong?"

"You never call on workdays." His matter-of-fact answer sent a wave of guilt over her. "How about not pretending with your old dad, and let me help?"

Tears sprang to her eyes.

"It's nothing, really. I just wanted to say hi."

"Is it about work? I saw the report you did at your sister's mission. If that doesn't get you the anchor job, those ninnies don't know real talent when they see it. I'm a little tired of watching that Kellie girl murdering the prompter. Did you hear her say the head of the school board 're-singed' instead of resigned? She's not quite the sharpest knife in the drawer is she?"

"Dad!" Laughter bubbled to her lips, and contentment lifted the gray from her mind at his loyalty. "Seriously, they haven't made a decision that I know of.

Kellie is doing much of the anchoring since Bruce's heart attack, but they've made it clear she's only pinch-hitting for now. So I guess we'll see."

"You'll get it. They'd be crazy not to give it to you."

"Thanks, Mac."

"So, let's talk about you coming home for the fall barbecue, right?"

A sudden longing washed over Raven. The picnic was two and a half full months away. That seemed too long.

"Actually, Dad, I thought I might come up for the Fourth of July. Do you have plans? I know it's only a week away, so if that's too short notice, I understand."

"Well, to tell you the truth, honey, Keri and Justin invited us—Ruthie and me—for the Fourth. So we'll be in Kansas City."

"Oh, I see." Rejection stung Raven. How could Keri plan a celebration and not invite Raven to join them? "That's great. Maybe you could stop by."

"Or you could join us. That brother-in-law of yours has gone and rounded up fifty barbecue grills and volunteers willing to barbecue. He's gotten permission from the store owners all around the mission to line up the grills on the sidewalk. They're going to be feeding the homeless hamburgers and hotdogs and chicken. They can't do fireworks in the city, but I'd wager those people haven't had a good barbecue in some time, if ever."

"That's great." Ambitious, perhaps.

"Ruthie is going to make her famous baked beans and coleslaw."

Guaranteed to give them all heartburn, no doubt, she thought uncharitably. But sheesh, how come Ruth got to be invited to this family thing and not Raven?

"You should come. Your sister could probably use the help."

Her sister could just lump it. How could she invite Dad for a holiday and completely leave her out? Once again she felt like a fifth wheel.

"I'll see what I can do, Dad. I'd better go. I'm about to get on the expressway. I'll need to pay attention to traffic."

"Okay, honey. I'll see you one way or another next weekend. If you don't show up at the mission, we'll drop by before we head home. Maybe we can have dinner."

"Sure."

Raven fought back tears and anger, disappointment and loneliness, as she entered the fray of cars weaving in and out of lanes of traffic.

Maybe Sonny was going to be the only real family she had after all.

Matthew sat across the desk from Stuart McBride at Healy and McBride's law offices.

"Do you honestly think you can go back to practicing law in this city, Matt?"

"Why not?"

"Why not indeed." Stuart chuckled. "What about our clients who disagree with your policies? You haven't made a secret of your stance on many controversial issues."

"Then I'd be great to represent those clients who do agree with me. Right?"

"Tell you what," Stuart said, leaning back in his brown leather chair. "How about giving me a few days to think about it and discuss it with my partners? Then I'll give you a call."

Disappointment clawed at Matthew's heart. Stuart didn't look very encouraging.

Matthew clenched his jaw as he walked toward the elevator. Wasn't there anything left for him? His law education. His political ambitions. There was nothing left. How did a thirty-seven-year-old man start all over?

He maneuvered in and out of traffic, instinct driving the car as much as Matthew. All he'd ever wanted to do was make a difference in his corner of the world.

What happened to a man once his dreams were crushed? When everything he'd ever thought he was meant to be suddenly seemed impossible?

Somehow, thirty minutes later, he found himself in Pastor Jim Hickman's office voicing the same questions.

The pastor steepled his fingers on his sleek mahogany desk. "So what you're saying is that suddenly your purpose in life has switched gears?"

Matthew nodded. "I always knew I'd follow in my father's footsteps and enter the political arena. There wasn't any question. As a kid, I was groomed that way, but I made the choice consciously as an adult. My parents' dreams became my own. I honestly believed God had directed me toward politics."

"And do you think God changed his mind?"

Matthew stared at the pastor, trying to wrap his mind around the question.

"Matt, the path before us isn't always without struggle. What if you'd run for senate and lost? Would you have tried again?"

"Of course."

"Then perhaps you need to look at this as a setback designed to strengthen you for the next phase of the battle." He slid his black, leather-bound Bible across the desk until it sat on the desk in front of him. He flipped through the pages. "David had God's promise that he'd be king from the time he was only a boy. But it didn't happen immediately, did it?"

"I guess not."

"After Samuel anointed David, David went right back to the fields to tend his sheep until the appointed time.

"His purpose was to be king. But his situation in life dictated that he tend sheep.

"Even when he finally made it to the palace, it was only to play his harp for the reigning king.

"David must have been excited to get that invitation, thinking, this is it. I'm going to play for the king and he'll make me his heir.

"Instead, Saul eventually hated him and David had to run for his life."

Matthew's heart began to lift with hope as Pastor Jim put the story into perspective for him and paralleled it to his own life.

The preacher rested his clasped hands on the white pages in front of him. "Sometimes God reveals what He's eventually planned for us to be, but we have to walk out the steps to get there. For David it was walking out the steps to the palace. He had to decide whether or not to believe the word that God had given him through Samuel even when it seemed as though he would never be king. If you truly believe that God has designed for you to be an elected official, then you can't let a little thing like being forced to pull out of your first primary discourage you."

"That little thing, huh?" Matthew drawled.

Pastor Jim's eyes lit with amusement. "It may not seem small now, but looking back on it someday, you'll be able to appreciate the lesson this step brings."

Matthew stood and offered his hand. Pastor Jim took it, but instead of releasing it immediately, he bowed his head and prayed for Matthew. A sense of peace enveloped Matthew's heart as the man sent up a petition filled with thanksgiving to God.

Matt drove home, renewed with confidence that whatever happened over the next few days or weeks or months—however long it took to find out who was harassing him, and to defuse Ray, if they were not the same man—that God did truly have a plan for him. His purpose, for now, was to take care of his daughter. To keep her safe and secure.

Why would Strong visit a church in the middle of a weekday? Did this have anything to do with Raven Mahoney? Did Strong think he was going to marry her and be one big happy family with the little girl?

He tasted the bitterness in his mouth as the image whirled around his mind. He pictured a little dark-headed girl, full of life and innocence. He'd been robbed of watching her grow up. But now that he'd seen her, touched her, he couldn't let anyone steal her away from him.

But Strong didn't seem to understand that.

He puffed reflectively on his cigarette.

How much more was he really expected to take? Apparently his dealings with Strong hadn't been forceful enough. E-mails, letters, even the threat of kidnapping—those hadn't been enough to convince him how serious this situation truly was. Time to step up the action and let him know this wasn't a game.

Chapter Fifteen

"Raven, Mr. Cruise wants to see you in his office."

Raven rolled her eyes and saved the copy she was working on for her new piece on school lunches. Were the choices on the menu healthy enough? Why were there so many fat kids in America? Was it really the school lunches or did parents need to turn off the TVs, computer and video games, and maybe make them play outside for a change?

She had to be careful not to voice her opinion on this one. Especially since her viewers knew she didn't have any kids. Statistics showed that sixty-five percent of their audience comprised households with two or more children. She couldn't appear to blame parents for the upward trend of childhood obesity. Even if the fault lay solely at their feet.

Irritation bit through her as she made her way to her boss's office. She tapped on his door then poked her head in. "You wanted to see me?"

"Yes." The pudgy, balding man looked every inch the newsman. He wore a button-down dress shirt with the sleeves rolled up mid forearm—very Lou Grant. "Come in, Raven. Close the door, will you?"

She did as requested and slipped into the chair he indicated. "What's up?"

"I need to talk to you about Bruce's job."

Raven's heart did a double take. She fought to maintain composure. "What about it?"

"As you know, he planned to retire at the end of the year, but his heart problems forced him to step down from his position earlier. He won't be coming back."

"I didn't expect that he would. That's too bad."

Get on with it. Just tell me your little Kellie—the apple of Daddy's eye—is getting the anchor so I can turn in my resignation and be done with it.

"I know everyone is upset about Kellie filling in." He caught her eye, daring her to deny it.

She nodded. "Kellie hasn't paid her dues the way the rest of us have. And to be honest, Mr. Cruise, even if I don't get Bruce's job, there are at least three others in line who are more qualified than your daughter."

There, let him get mad and fire her. She'd collect unemployment while she lined up another news job.

He gathered in a long breath and blew it out in what could only be described as frustration. "I know she isn't qualified or ready. The kid is only twenty-four. She hasn't had a number-one news story, even. To tell you the truth, the only reason I let her fill in was because she begged me to let her give it a shot and her mother went to bat for her."

"Ah, so they ganged up on you." Raven's lips twitched with amusement at this newly exposed human side of Mr. Cruise. It almost made her like him. At any rate, she could sympathize—a little.

"*Ganged up* is precisely what they did. I knew I

couldn't give Kellie the position permanently, but I figured it might not hurt anything to let her get her feet wet. Just for a little while until I made my decision as to who actually gets the job permanently."

Raven stared at him, suddenly sorry she'd ever called him a weasel. This was a dad, loving his daughter, and not wanting to hurt her.

"So, we've made our decision and would like to offer you the job. With your potential, I don't know why you've stayed at Channel 23 as long as you have, but ratings polls show you are a consistent favorite with our viewers. The terms are laid out in the contract. Go over it and see what you think. Let us know. We'd like to introduce you as the permanent anchor next Monday on the evening news."

"I—I don't know what to say. Honestly. I can't believe it."

He nodded. "It probably wasn't fair to you not to ask you immediately." He gave her a sheepish grin. "Chalk it up to fatherly weakness."

Raven smiled indulgently as she stood, taking the contract with her. "I'll read this over and get back to you soon."

"I'll look forward to hearing your thoughts on it." He walked her to the door. "What I don't look forward to is living with my wife and daughter for the next few days. By the way, we're rerunning the piece you did on the little girl. Ratings shot up on that one. I'd like you to go over there and do a follow-up for tomorrow's six o'clock news."

Hesitating only a moment at the resentment still hanging on over Keri's failure to invite her for the Fourth of July barbecue at the mission, Raven the professional emerged strong and nodded. "I'll grab Ken and get right on it."

Raven left the office, clutching the contract to her chest. She couldn't resist the smile forming on her lips.

The job was hers! Without Matt's story, without a fight. Something had finally gone her way. She walked back to her office, conscious that her shoulders were a little straighter, her chin lifted with new confidence.

She caught movement in her periphery and turned, connecting eye to eye with Kellie across the room. The girl's thin, perfectly arched brows narrowed. Then her blue eyes widened as apparent understanding dawned. Her face reddened. She looked toward her father's office, then started toward it, determination increasing visibly with every jerky stride.

Poor Mr. Cruise. Raven wouldn't be in his shoes for anything in the world.

She closed her office door and glanced about. Now what? Good news was meant to be shared with loved ones. But she hadn't spoken to anyone in her family for three days, not since the evening of her dinner with Sonny.

She studied the phone on her desk, tapping her nails on the numbers, debating whether or not to call Matt. He hadn't called her since that wonderful kiss in this very office three days ago. What if he didn't want to talk to her?

Making a snap decision, she grabbed up the phone and punched in Matt's home phone number. After four rings, she was about to hang up when Mrs. Strong answered, sounding out of breath.

"Hello, is Matthew there, please?"

"Raven, is that you?" Her voice didn't exactly exude warmth, but neither was she cool. Detached, wary. And Raven didn't blame her.

Raven swallowed hard. "Yes, ma'am."

"Matthew took Jamie and went on a little vacation.

I'm surprised he didn't call you. You two seem to be…close these days."

"Do we?" Reeling from the knowledge that Matthew had left town without bothering to let her know, Raven fought to keep her tone even.

"Aren't you?"

"I don't know if *close* is exactly the right word. We've only been back in contact for a couple of weeks, so it isn't surprising that he wouldn't consult me about his plans."

"I see. Well, my son will be home this weekend for the fireworks display at the fairgrounds, so I will let him know you called. I expect you'll be hearing from him."

"It's not important. Please don't bother him about it. Goodbye, Mrs. Strong."

"Goodbye, then."

Disappointment clutched at Raven's belly. How could Matt kiss her like that and then just take off for parts unknown without so much as a little phone call?

She dialed Ken's cell phone. A feminine voice answered. "Ken's phone," she said with a giggle.

"Give me that phone, girl," Ken boomed from the background. "No one answers my phone but me, Kellie-girl."

Kellie? Disgusted, Raven disconnected the call. Kellie must have run right to Ken after her talk with Mr. Cruise. He'd certainly cheered her up quickly enough. The catty girl had to try to get everything that belonged to Raven—even her cameraman.

She snatched up her purse and her new contract, and headed for the door. She needed to get out of here.

On the way to her car, she spied Ken and Kellie, locked in an embrace next to his beater of a pickup. Tears stung her eyes. How much more could she lose and still hold it together? Loneliness nearly overwhelmed her.

"Raven! Rave, wait up."

She turned at the sound of Ken's voice, her defenses raised and gearing for a fight. "If you're finished making out with the boss's daughter," she said, not caring how testy she sounded, "we have work to do down at Victory Mission. Frank wants a follow-up on Anaya's story."

Ken's lined face scrunched into a frown. "Hey, what's with the attitude? You sound like a jealous wife—and believe me, I've had four of them so I should know." He adjusted his camera bag over his shoulder. "I just heard the news. Congratulations, kiddo. I never doubted you for a second."

"Do you really mean it? Or were you pulling for Kellie all along?"

"You mean that little kiss?" He sent her a rakish grin. "That was just a consolation prize."

"Little kiss, my big toe." Raven scowled and folded her arms across her chest. "If that was a little kiss, I'd like to see a big one."

His eyebrow rose. "I'd oblige if you weren't so much like my own little sister." He reached out and ruffled her hair, then laughed outright when she swatted his hand away.

"Ha! You'd be the last man on earth I'd kiss anyway. I might as well grab an ashtray and kiss it." Raven opened her SUV door. "Are you coming?"

Three days at the lake had done wonders for Matt's nerves. At their secluded family cabin, he'd been able to relax. From his family's private beach, he watched his daughter splashing about in the water, carefree and full of innocence, blissfully unaware that a man might want to cause her harm, or at the very least, use her for his own financial gain.

The thought clenched his gut and the familiar feeling of helplessness invaded his heart. If only they could stay away from the world forever. But he knew that wasn't possible. Jamie had ball games and he had to settle his relationship with Raven.

He couldn't figure out why she hadn't returned any of his calls. He'd even driven by her house and slipped a note under her door to let her know he was leaving and to give the address where she could reach him in case she wanted to drive up to the lake for a day. But no word.

From the cabin, he heard the jangling of the phone and hopped to his feet. "James! Get out of the water for a few minutes and rest on the beach, I'm going inside to answer the phone."

"Oh, man! Can't I stay in?"

"No," he called over his shoulder. "Get out now."

The phone rang with persistence. Maybe his thoughts had conjured Raven to call him. A grin played at his lips. "Hello?"

"Jamie looks sweet lying on the beach." The distorted voice laughed. Evil. Purposeful.

"Who is this? Ray?"

"You really shouldn't leave her alone like that. You never know who might be watching."

"What do you want from me? More money?"

"You might be able to put a price on family, Strong. But not me."

"You're not going to get her away from me. Do you hear me? No matter what I have to do."

The line went dead. Snatching his cell phone from the charger by the door, Matt sprinted onto the porch and down the cabin steps. Jamie lay on the beach, so still… His imagination went into overdrive. "Jamie!" To his relief, the little girl sat up. "Yeah, Dad?"

He rushed to her side and gathered her into his arms.

"Hey!" she groused, wriggling free. "What's up with that? You about smothered me."

"Sorry. I just needed a hug."

"Well, ask next time so I can be ready." She grinned and flung her arms around his neck in a stranglehold, stealing his heart and his breath. "There. Can I go back into the water now?"

"No. You need to come inside so we can clean the cabin and pack up. We're going home in the morning."

"A day early?"

"Yeah. Do you mind?"

She gave a little shrug of bony sun-kissed shoulders. "To tell you the truth, I was starting to get a little bored with just you to play with."

"Hey, thanks a lot, sport. Maybe I'm overdue for some adult conversation too. Ever think of that?"

A snort blew through her. "You mean like Raven?"

"Maybe."

"Grams said she better not break your heart again, or else."

"Or else what?"

"She didn't say. Just said 'or else.'"

"I see…" He was going to have to have a word with his mother about what were considered proper topics of conversation with Jamie.

Jamie reached down and snatched up her soggy towel from the sandy beach. "Let's clean up. Can we make a campfire later and roast hot dogs and marshmallows?"

"Sounds great."

He held the binoculars to his eyes, watching father and daughter walking toward the cabin. He had to shake his head. Strong was a class-A idiot. Why didn't it occur to the guy that he was watching the little girl from a boat on the lake?

Their beach might be private, but the water didn't belong to the Strong family. He'd debated whether to pull the boat in close and snatch up Jamie from the water, just to prove he could, but that was too risky. He wasn't going to play many more games. Strong had made it clear he wouldn't give up without a fight.

So, the gloves were off now? This might be fun.

Chapter Sixteen

Raven felt chubby hands climbing up her leg and she glanced down. Anaya's beautiful brown face looked up and her arms lifted, eliciting a smile from Raven's lips.

"Hey there, doll," she said pulling the child into her arms. "I think you're even more gorgeous today than you were last time I saw you."

The toddler responded to Raven's friendly tone with a giggle. Her face split into a grin. She held up two fingers. "Two?"

"Two? Two what?"

"She's telling you that's how old she is." Keri's husky, amusement-filled voice preceded her into Raven's personal space.

So far she'd had very little to say to her sister, who *still* hadn't brought up the barbecue. But who could even think resentful thoughts while holding such perfection in one's arms?

"No calls yet?" she asked.

Keri smoothed the little girl's pigtails. "None."

The sorrow in her sister's round brown eyes touched Raven's heart. "Don't give up. It's been less than a week. Maybe this time around the clip will get into the right hands."

"I hope so, Rave. I don't know how long they'll let me keep her. A beauty like Anaya will be so easy to place for adoption. I've prayed and prayed, but I can't help but feel like there's no point in airing this story in Missouri. Mary wasn't from around here. It's just not likely that anyone from her past will recognize her."

"What if her real family isn't a good choice to raise her? It's possible they're druggies or worse. Why did Mary run off?"

"No. It wasn't like that. Mary was a victim of an on-line predator. She was only fourteen and this guy started talking to her through instant messages and e-mail. After a while some of their e-mails back and forth were pretty graphic. Her parents were strict Christians and found out about it. Of course they immediately forbade any further contact and took away the Internet, but it was too late. By then, they'd talked on the phone a couple of times. She went to meet him one night and he kidnapped her, raped her and drove her here to Kansas City where he kept her tied up in a seedy motel. It was only by the grace of God that he didn't kill her. One day he just left and didn't come back. The owner of the motel found her tied to the bed after three days with no food or water. She thought she was being rescued. Instead he turned out to be a pimp. He got her well and put her to work."

Keri's eyes were filled with tears by the time she finished the story. "Mary's greatest prayer was that her daughter never ever have to taste the street life. She was this close to calling home, Raven! This close." The frustration flowed from deep inside Keri, the problem solver. The one who always made things happen. "If only we could get this out!"

Anaya yawned and laid her chubby cheek against Raven's shoulder. Raven pressed a kiss on the soft skin. "If I were Katie Couric, I'd get this little girl on the *Today* show tomorrow."

Keri gave her a watery smile. "I know you would, Raven. I appreciate all you've done. Don't think I don't, okay? I'm just afraid we're wasting our time."

"Rave," Ken's voice broke into the conversation as he filled the doorway to Keri's office. "You about ready to wrap this up? We should get back to the station."

"All right. Here, take her, she's starting to drool on my shirt anyway."

A laugh bubbled from Keri's lips. "You loved every second of holding that warm, sweet baby in your arms."

"You'll never get me to confess," Raven said with mock determination. "Shoot me, beat me, boil me in oil, I'll never admit to wanting one of my own."

She stopped short, her own shock reflected on her sister's face. "Well, then," Keri said. "That was more than I would have guessed. Looks like running into ol' Matthew again is starting to bring out your Molly-Homemaker side. I just knew it was in there somewhere." She laughed.

Raven squelched her irritation at her own slip of the tongue and rolled her eyes. "Don't order my wedding dress just yet, little sister."

"Well, that'll be a relief to poor Dad. Can you imagine marrying off three daughters in less than three years? Not to mention his own wedding if Ruth ever talks him into actually taking the long walk down the aisle."

Raven bristled at the very sound of Ruth's name. "If we're lucky, she never will."

Keri scowled. "I don't get why you have such a problem with Ruth."

"I don't get why you *don't* have a problem with her."

"For one thing, Dad's crazy about her. She's good for him. She makes him laugh."

"She sure isn't Mom," Raven muttered.

"No, she's not. She's Ruth and she makes Dad laugh. I remember how he laughed at Mom's silliness. Don't you?"

"Yeah."

"He has that same tender affection for Ruth. Sure, her Texas eccentricity can be overpowering at times, but her heart is as big as her home state and believe me, she makes him happy. You might as well accept it, because I'd be surprised if they aren't married by the end of the year."

"Raven! You coming or not?" Ken's impatience usually grated on Raven like a squeaky shopping cart, but this time his grumpy insistence came as a welcome excuse to boogie on out of there before she said something she'd regret.

"All right. I have to go, Kere-Bear."

"Wait, before you go. I have to tell you something."

Raven snatched up her purse from Keri's desk. "Tell me what?"

"Dad and Ruth are coming tomorrow for the weekend."

"I know. Dad told me when I called home the other night."

"You called Dad? Is everything okay?"

"That's an insulting implication."

"Well, you have to admit…"

"Oh, all right. I don't call Dad enough, but in this case, I just called to say hi and he told me about your little get-together."

Keri laughed. "I wouldn't exactly call it little. Probably every man, woman and child within a four-mile radius is going to show up for barbecue."

Everyone except me.

"Anyway, I didn't figure you'd want to come help out, but Justin said I should ask. Would you care to offer your wonderful services to help feed the poor?"

"Actually, Justin's right. I'd love to come and help out." A sense of relief streamed through Raven's body. She smiled and gave her sister a one-armed hug. "What time will you start barbecuing?"

"We won't actually until Saturday, but Dad and Ruth are coming tomorrow so that we can prepare the meat and side dishes. Want to come help with that?"

Raven walked toward the door. "I think I'll pass on that one," she tossed over her shoulder. "See you on Saturday."

"Be here early. By eight at least. We have a lot of meat to cook. I imagine people will start lining up pretty early and come through more than once."

"All right. I'll be here by eight."

Ken growled at her when she met him outside. "'Bout time. I had to circle the block four times."

"Sorry."

"I should have let that gang of hooligans have your hubcaps. That would serve you right."

"Sheesh, you are a grouch. And chuck the cigarette out the window. You know I don't let anyone smoke in here."

He took one last, long suck and flicked it out the window. "Happy?"

"Very." She tossed him a smug grin. "Hey Ken, do you know anyone who works for network news?"

A short laugh shot from his lips. "If I did, would I be working at a local cable channel?"

"How should I know?" Her defenses rose at the possible slight to the channel where she just happened to be the new anchor. Where was his loyalty?

"Why do you ask, anyway?"

Raven lifted her feet and rested her knees and shins on the front dash while she sank down in her seat. "Keri thinks we might be wasting time airing the segments in Missouri. She thinks Mary's parents live in a whole other state."

"Don't tell Frank. He loves this bleeding-heart stuff. Besides viewers are calling and e-mailing like crazy."

"I know. But what's the point in airing something that isn't going to do any good?"

"Are you serious?" Ken tossed her an incredulous look before focusing back on traffic.

Raven nodded.

"Ratings?" Ken shrugged. "I don't know. If I had a way to get this out for you, I would, you know."

"I know you would, Ken. And I appreciate the thought." Raven smiled and touched his hand. It wasn't often she caught a glimpse of Ken's gentle side, but at times like this, she knew he cared about her. "I guess we need a miracle."

Ken's cynical laugh filled the SUV but stopped as abruptly as it had begun. "What? You mean you're seriously going to pray for a miracle?"

Raven shrugged. "I don't know. Maybe. As a last resort."

"Never thought I'd see the day, little girl."

Raven didn't answer. Rather, she turned to stare out at the traffic, not really seeing anything as her thoughts took her upward.

Here's one for you God. How about getting this story out on a national level? Help me help this little girl and I'll... Raven conjured up the image of Anaya's sweet face. *I'll go to church again on Sunday.*

* * *

Matthew sat at his desk, glad to be home. He clicked on his e-mail and scrolled through the spam, forwards and other junk mail. He stopped scrolling and opened an e-mail with the subject line: Anaya

A smile lifted the corners of his lips as he reached for the phone.

Raven slammed in the door and tossed her keys on the counter. She'd spent the entire afternoon editing the piece from the mission, unable to shake the deal she'd made with God. She knew better. God didn't make deals. It was His way or the highway.

"Come on, Ginger, let's go watch TV." She reached for her stuffed cat and stopped short. Ginger's chair was empty? When did Ginger get up and slink away?

Must have left Ginger in the living room. "Here, kitty, kitty," she said with a grin. No sign of Ginger. Bedroom? After checking every room possible, Raven's humor turned sour. Where could the stuffed cat have gone?

Had someone broken in? Panic gave her a nudge. She began a thorough search of anything valuable. Digital camera? Check. Laptop? Check. Mother's princess cut diamond engagement ring and ruby necklace? Check. DVD player, VCR, TV, camcorder. Everything sat in its proper place, mocking her with the absurdity of the idea that someone might have actually stolen her thirty-year-old stuffed cat instead of something with resale value.

She spent the next half hour combing every inch of her house. Finally, she plopped dejectedly onto her sofa. She had no choice but to conclude that her beloved childhood toy was lost. She must have stuck it away in a box somewhere by mistake during one of her sporadic periods of cleaning. Ugh. She'd been so distracted lately. There was no telling where it was.

Suddenly only chocolate would do. Lots of it. A blissful chocolate fest wouldn't bring Ginger back, but it would definitely take her into oblivion for the time being. She shoved herself up from the couch and headed into the kitchen to snag some rocky road ice cream. The flashing light on her answering machine caught her eye. She pressed the button and continued to the freezer.

"Raven. It's Sonny. I'll call again later."

Beep.

"Hi, Raven. It's Sonny again. I guess you're still not home."

Beep.

"Raven. Are you there? You're not ignoring me, are you?"

Sheesh, Sonny. Don't you have a life?

Beep.

"Raven, it's Matt. Judging from the fact that you never returned my call or acknowledged my note, I guess you don't want anything to do with me. But I have some news you are definitely going to want to hear. Call me."

Raven stopped short. "Note?" She stared at the answering machine as though it held any answers for her. "What note are you talking about, Matt?"

The clock on her microwave flashed ten-thirty, by all rights too late for anyone with a shred of politeness to make a phone call. And she never would call his home phone that late because his mother or Jamie would most likely be in bed. But she wasn't above taking a chance that he might be lying in bed watching late-night TV.

Without a second thought, she reached for the phone and dialed his cell.

He picked up on the first ring. "Raven?"

"Yes. I just got your message. What note?"

"What?"

"The note you left. I never got one. And I didn't get any messages from you, either."

"Seriously?"

"I promise. I never received either."

"That explains why I didn't hear from you while I was up at the lake with Jamie."

"I'm glad you tried to contact me before you left. I thought…"

"That I kissed and ran away like Georgie Porgie?"

Raven's heart lifted at the humor in his voice. "Something like that."

"I already told you my position won't change. I wrote a note telling you I was going out of town and inviting you to join us for a day at the lake."

A rush of heat flooded through her. "I would have enjoyed that."

"Me too."

Silence reigned between them until Raven cleared her throat and got back to the matter at hand. "So, Matt. What news do you have for me?"

"Oh, I sent your piece about Anaya to a friend of mine in New York. He likes your presence and thinks Anaya's story is worth pursuing nationally."

Raven's heart skipped a beat. "Are you serious? Matt! Network news?"

"Yep. He's going to call your boss and get it all set up."

"Do you realize Anaya will have a chance to grow up with her own family if this works?"

"Do you realize you didn't mention what this could do for your career?"

"Think it's character growth?"

Laughter rumbled from Matt's chest. "Could be."

Anaya's sweet face crept to Raven's mind. She grinned to herself. *So, You took me up on my challenge, huh, God? I guess I should have made the deal that Anaya has to find her family before I go to church again.*

But that wasn't the deal. And there was only one thing she could do. "Matt. How would you like to pick me up for church on Sunday?"

The old stuffed cat winked at him from its perch on the sofa. By now Raven Mahoney should have figured out that someone had been in her apartment. She would know he'd taken the one thing she cherished the most.

A sense of satisfaction engulfed him that he'd pulled it off. So far, Matthew Strong hadn't been so great at taking a hint. But the guy would have to know how serious he was this time.

Chapter Seventeen

After a night of barely sleeping, Raven stumbled into the station carrying an extra large double-chocolate mocha latte. Who needed sleep? She was riding on an adrenaline rush directly related to Matt's news.

Frank Cruise met her at the door. "I thought I told you to take a few days off." His poorly concealed smile belied the gruffness of his tone and Raven knew he'd received the phone call from Matthew's contact in New York. He jerked his head toward his office. "Let's talk."

She practically floated behind him and slid into the chair across the cluttered desk from his. For the first five minutes, she waited impatiently while he told her what she already knew. The network liked her tape, loved the story, wanted to take it to a national level and see what might happen in Anaya's case. "So? What's the bottom line?"

"So the network wants to do the overdubs, but will use yours and Ken's footage."

Raven's heart sank. If they weren't going to use her face and voice, it meant no move to New York, no network job.

Funny how only yesterday she was on top of the

world for landing the anchor spot. Mentally, she gave herself a sound smack. God had obviously been willing to go to some lengths to get her to go to church. She should have held out for a network job.

"I'm sorry you seem to be disappointed. But this is great for the station. They're going to mention our call letters and station number. And that means potentially a lot more viewers."

"Then I'm glad I haven't signed that contract yet. Looks like this might have made me a little more valuable to the station than the deal you've offered."

A *V* formed between his eyes. "Don't get too cocky. Remember it's your story they want. Not you."

Stung by the comment, Raven nevertheless rose from the chair with dignity. "Yet," she tossed over her shoulder, just before exiting the office.

Her intercom was buzzing by the time she got to her own office. "Yes?"

"You didn't give me a chance to finish," Frank's voice huffed through the machine like Darth Vader with a whine.

"Sorry." She lifted her heavy hair from her neck and piled it atop her head, holding it there. "Go ahead."

"The network is sending a team tomorrow and would like you to meet them at the mission. They want to look around, interview your sister for themselves."

"Keri's never going to agree to that, she's planning an Independence Day barbecue for all the homeless down there." Grim satisfaction and just a little feeling of justice fought for attention. She shoved them back, but couldn't resist a tiny grin.

Oblivious to her moment of victory, Frank pushed the issue with all the vigor of a man with something to lose. "That's the point. She's already turned them down. But

I happened to mention your—uh—familial relationship with the people who run the mission and the network hoped you'd persuade them otherwise. Either way, they're coming."

"Frank!" Frustration nipped at the edges of Raven's already sleep-deprived nerves. Her hair cascaded down her back as she dropped her hands and slapped the desk with her palms. "Keri isn't going to want the media making a spectacle of this. She doesn't do anything for attention."

"Boy, she's not a bit like you, then, is she? What, was she adopted?"

"No, she wasn't as a matter of fact. I was!" Raven snapped, then gasped at her admission. "I—I'll call her."

"Hey, Raven, I didn't mean to…"

Raven shut off the intercom. A fifteen-year-old secret, and the first person she shared it with was a middle-aged, balding weasel of a spineless news director.

Raven leaned forward across her desk and rested her forehead on her folded arms. This day was supposed to be charmed. She wasn't supposed to feel depressed. The little office suddenly began to close in around her. Her breath came in short bursts. "I gotta get out of here."

So she had no work to do today, according to Frank, other than convince Keri to put hundreds of homeless and hungry on display. Still, she had to admit the story might actually be a good thing. The attention it could bring not only Anaya but the mission itself could potentially bring in more donations. As always, her mind began to whirl with the new idea, and a rush of adrenaline shot through her veins, giving her a burst of energy.

She snatched up her keys. Keri wouldn't be as likely to brush her off if she had to look her in the eye.

* * *

"Hey, I thought you weren't coming until tomorrow." Keri's pleased greeting sent a rush of warmth through Raven. The sight of her sister's face, flushed with pleasure, brought a smile to her lips and put her instantly at ease.

"I had the day off."

Keri waved her to the small break table in a corner of the massive kitchen. She grabbed the coffeepot and two mugs from the cabinet. Sitting across from Raven, she poured the steaming brew and set the pot on the table. "How'd you manage to get off work on a Friday?"

"Actually, the powers that be offered me Bruce's job. I'm supposed to be considering the contract this weekend." She shook two pink packets of artificial sweetener and dumped the contents into her cup. "They must be pretty sure I'm going to sign, though, because they plan for me to start Monday."

Keri darted from her seat and caught Raven in a stranglehold. "Rave! How incredible. I'm so proud of you." The old Keri hadn't been so demonstrative. Justin's love and becoming mother to his twin ten-year-old sons had definitely brought out a more open side of Keri. She slid back into her chair, her face beaming with pure joy. "You deserve it, you know?"

"I suppose."

"What do you mean you suppose?"

"There are others who might think they deserve it more."

"Well, they don't." Keri's choppy words left no room for argument.

Keri's expression grew serious and she followed the rim of her cup with her index finger. "Hey, Rave. I got a call this morning. Did you already know that?"

Raven's gaze faltered beneath her sister's. She nodded. "Frank asked me to come down and talk some sense into you."

Keri's freckles scrunched together as her red-headed Irish temper shot to the surface. "I should have known you wouldn't come just to share your news with me. That would be too sentimental, wouldn't it?" She snatched up her cup and dumped the coffee into the sink. "I have work to do before the lunch crowd shows up."

Raven watched Keri's jerky movements, half expecting her sister to continue to lash out verbally. But she remained silent. A scolding, Raven could have defended, but silent rebuke only raised her defenses without giving her any real ammo.

"Listen. Think whatever you want. The truth is, yes, Frank asked me to talk to you, but no, I didn't have to come down here. I have a phone in my office, a phone in my house and a cell phone. We both have e-mail, and if all else fails there's a pay phone in the station I could have used if I'd wanted to."

"Don't give me that," Keri growled without even hesitating to take in Raven's words. "You've said a hundred times that you need to really look someone in the eye to get your point across."

Heat rushed to Raven's cheeks. "All right. That's true. And I did want to talk to you face-to-face. But not so that I could weasel you into agreeing to this."

"Why does your career advancement always have to come first? Can't you for once put people ahead of your own needs?" Keri leaned against the sink, facing Raven, her hands resting on the stainless steel behind her. "I suppose you're eyeing a job with a national news station?"

"Okay, actually, the network is using my angle on the

story and Ken's footage, but that's about it. They aren't using me to do the report." She stood, her knees trembling from the emotionally charged conversation. "Happy?"

"What do you mean, they're using your story, but not you? That's not fair."

"They feel the story holds appeal, but they don't want me. So you see, my motives are pure as the driven snow. And if you don't let them do the story, then I guess my deal with God is off and I can sleep in Sunday morning."

Keri gave her a wary frown. "What deal?"

"I asked for national coverage for Anaya's story. With the promise that I'd go to church Sunday if He came through. But no story, no church."

Laughter bubbled from Keri's lips. "Are you trying to imply that if I don't let you do the story I'm somehow thwarting God's plan for Anaya?"

Raven shrugged. "I did my part. God did His. You're the only hold-up on this one. Where is Anaya, anyway?"

"My office. We brought some stuff for her. The boys are babysitting." She shifted from one foot to the other, her hand resting squarely on her hip. "How can I exploit these people?"

"Look at this less as exploitation and more as an opportunity for Anaya." Raven strode across the floor, her tennis shoes squeaking on the shining tiles. "Think about what this could mean for the mission if people consider it a cause for donation. Remember what happened to Denni's house after we aired that story on our small local cable channel? This is national, Kere-Bear. Think about how many homes will hear about the work you're doing here."

Indecision played across Keri's face. "I'll have to talk it over with Justin."

"The news crew will be here tomorrow, so make it quick."

"All right. I'll talk to him right after lunch. On one condition…"

"What's that?"

"Stay and help us serve lunch."

Raven grinned. "You're on."

"I don't see why I can't go too, Dad." Jamie perched on the edge of the sink and watched Matthew slather shaving cream on his face.

"Because it's not the place for a kid, that's why."

During a two-hour conversation with Raven the night before, Matt had discovered several things: One, Raven had spent the day dishing up food for the needy; two, she'd failed to mention her promotion, an omission he'd decided to attribute to her new character growth translated into humility; and three, today, she would be on hand to dole out hot dogs and hamburgers to give people who never had the chance at homemade barbecue to experience a little taste of the good life. And four, Raven might be having more of a spiritual crisis than he'd originally believed. Most people had periods of time where they neglected Bible study or prayer for a little while. That would be enough to explain a spiritual cooling-off. But Raven seemed bitter. For instance, when he'd mentioned how God had obviously brought little Anaya to the mission, she'd glibly said, "Maybe, but you'd think God would have just kept her mom out of the path of a drive-by shooting in the first place." Little things like that were beginning to make Matthew wonder if perhaps Raven was going through more than a cooling-off period. Sometimes she seemed downright cold.

Still, he wanted to be near her. And the opportunity

to serve the poor had compelled him to hint shamelessly until she'd finally invited him to help. But that didn't mean he was willing to risk Ray snatching Jamie.

"What do you mean it's not a place for kids? Raven said her nephews help all the time."

"That's because their parents run the place."

"Well, what about the poor kids?"

"You are not a poor kid. There's no reason for you to be there."

"Miss Cindy taught us about the Good Samaritan in Sunday school last week. She said it's everyone's place to look out for people who need our help."

Matthew finished rinsing his razor and set it on the counter. He patted his face dry, conscious that he was stalling. How did he convince her to stop pestering him to go down to the mission, but still reiterate the fact that her Sunday-school teacher was absolutely right. It definitely seemed like an inconsistency on his part.

Raising a kid right wasn't easy. But how could he put her in possible harm's way? He knew Justin and Keri had been keeping an eye out for Ray since last Sunday, but so far, there had been no sign of him. Perhaps it had been a one-time thing.

"Please, Dad." Jamie's voice pulled him from his thoughts. "I really want to help."

"Why is this so important to you, honey?" He lifted her from the counter and carried her into the bedroom where he sat on a chair, cradling her close.

She shrugged. "I was thinking about the little girl whose mom died last week and how she might have to go to a foster home if they can't find her family pretty soon."

"What do you think you can do for Anaya, James?"

"It's not that. I just thought…" She gathered a shaky breath and looked up at him with soulful eyes. "What if you and Grams didn't know about me when I was born? What if Aunt Casey didn't have a place to live?"

Now he understood. *There but for the grace of God, go I.*

He brushed her cheek and fought back tears. How did an eight-year-old child even have the understanding to recognize such a truth? There could only be one explanation: God had revealed it to her.

"All right, sport. You win. But stay close to me. You hear?"

Her joyful response was muffled as she squirmed around to hug him close.

Matthew knew as soon as he saw the lines forming for the barbecue that he'd made the right decision to bring his daughter down here. Fear had gnawed at him from the time he'd consented, and he'd almost changed his mind. But something about her simple explanation made him feel as though perhaps God had a purpose for her coming, if for no other reason than just to see how blessed they were. Holding tightly to Jamie's hand, he made his way through the private entrance in the back.

"Ease up on my hand, Dad. You're about to squeeze it off."

"Sorry." He loosened his grip, but wasn't quite ready to let go completely.

"Matthew, Jamie, you made it!" Raven greeted them when they entered the kitchen area where several volunteers labored over pots of baked beans, corn on the cob, and ovens of brownies and cookies.

His heart rejoiced at the sight of her. How could he have missed her so much in the span of just a few days? And how could she have gotten even more breathtakingly beautiful in the same amount of time?

A flush stole across Raven's cheeks as he brushed a quick kiss across her lips.

"Oh, brother. Not in public, Dad."

Raven smiled down at Jamie. "How's soccer coming along, Jamie?"

"Undefeated."

"Great. You getting any play time?"

Matthew's lips twitched as Jamie bristled. The little girl shook loose from him and folded her arms across her chest. She lifted her chin and blew an enormous bubble with her gum, then sucked it in with a loud pop. "MVP for the last three games."

Raven's brow rose with the appropriate amazement. "Wow. That calls for a celebration. How about a soda?" She reached into an ice-filled aluminum tub and grabbed a can.

Never one to hold a grudge, Jamie reached for the offering. "Thanks."

"Raven, honey," a booming voice called across the kitchen. "Keri says will you bring that other tub of coleslaw?"

"I'm right on it, Dad."

"It'll be nice to see your dad again."

"Yeah. He always liked you." Raven hefted a large tub from the stainless-steel industrial refrigerator.

Matthew took the slaw from her. Something he couldn't quite put his finger on had dampened her mood at the mere mention of introducing him to Mac.

"Hey, you don't have to introduce us. I'll stay out of the way."

"Don't be silly. Dad's anxious to meet 'the one that got away.'"

"I didn't get away. I was just put on the shelf and forgotten for a while." He looked deeply into her eyes, willing her to give him a glimpse of the emotions lying below the surface.

A soft smile touched her lips and she placed a warm palm on his cheek. "Not forgotten, Matt. Not even for a second."

So help him, if he wasn't carrying twenty pounds of cabbage, carrots and mayo, he'd whisk her away to the first minister they could find and make this thing legal right now.

"Today, Raven!"

"Coming, Dad." She dropped her tone. "Sheesh, he's a veritable Job isn't he?"

A chuckle rumbled in his chest. "A study in patience."

She rolled her eyes. "Follow me, Muscles."

Matt turned to Jamie. "Come on and let's see what Miss Keri has for you to do."

Raven tossed the girl a mock warning glance. "My sister's a real slave driver. You sure you know what you're getting yourself into?"

Jamie nodded. "I'm ready to roll up my sleeves and do some good in this world."

Tenderness washed over Matthew. The philosophies that had made his father a great politician had obviously made a bigger impression on his daughter than Matt ever knew.

The surprise in Raven's eyes was understandable. She'd never heard Senator James Strong just before he embarked on a new community service project. But Jamie had. And Matthew had over and over as a kid. Public service was part of his heritage. Something his heart couldn't deny. He stared out at the crowd gathering around. Careworn faces of men and women who could have been thirty or sixty for all he could tell. For most, poverty and hard living had taken their toll, robbing these people of youth and vitality. Undernourished children eyed the food hungrily and parents whose hopelessness weighed down slumped shoulders averted their eyes rather than make contact and risk rejection.

These were his people. The ones he wanted to help, was destined to help. Justin and Keri had embraced the hands-on everyday calling of ministry. Following the Great Commission. Feeding the body and soul. But Matthew knew he could help on a legislative level.

His daughter would be part of it. And unless he missed his guess, she'd be serving in her own capacity somehow.

He watched her literally roll up her sleeves and get to work. Pride swelled his chest as she smiled at a shy, blond boy who held out his plate for a hot dog.

"Good, you made it out here with that coleslaw." A massive hand clapped him on his shoulder. "Nice to see you again Matthew."

"Matthew Strong. Nice to see you again as well, Mr. Mahoney."

"Call me Mac. Take that tub out and put the new one in. Then go back and wash the old one. Don't forget to use the bleach-water rinse. Health code. We'll catch up later."

"Yes, sir." Matthew grinned and prepared himself to take orders for the rest of the day. He could certainly see where Raven got her bossiness.

He took the tub and turned toward the swinging kitchen doors. As he swung about, his eyes did a scan of the room. He stopped dead in his tracks. His heart did a double take and his palms began to sweat.

Cameras. Directed at Jamie. Smiling faces of newspeople who knew an adorable, sweet girl when they saw one. One of the women squatted down and asked her a question with the tape rolling. Matthew set the empty tub on the closest table and beelined for his daughter, his heart slamming against his chest. He reached her just in time to hear Jamie say, "My dad's Matthew Strong. He was almost going to be senator like my gramps. But he decided not to."

"Jamie." He glared at the reporter. "Stop the cameras. You can't tape my daughter without my permission."

"Actually, we can, Mr. Strong." She sized him up with frank perusal. "And what I've seen in the last fifteen minutes blows me away. That girl of yours exudes confidence, compassion, genuine caring without a lick of superiority. I'm amazed. Our viewers are going to love her. You should be proud of her."

"Listen." Matthew's voice went hoarse with fear. "You can't put my daughter's face on the air."

"Why, did you kidnap her? Afraid her real parents might find her?"

Indignation filled his chest until he realized the reporter was grinning. "Kidding."

But this wasn't a laughing matter as far as he was concerned.

"Look, we won't use her name and we won't show the two of you together so no one will make the connection. Feel better?"

"No."

"Hey, I'd like to help you out, but when my editor sees this footage, there's no way he's going to pass on it. Unless something better comes along."

"I thought you were here to talk about Anaya."

The woman nodded. "We are. And we'll be getting more footage today and will conduct an interview with the people who run this place, but throwing a huge block-party barbecue for the homeless is exactly what we'd like to show to go with it. It gives these people even more credibility. America loves human-interest stories."

"Find another human besides my daughter for America to be interested in." He whipped around, ready to grab Jamie and head for home. He wanted to help, but not at the risk that Ray might see her and try to get his fifteen minutes of fame to push his allegation that Matthew's family had somehow coerced him into signing away his rights to Jamie.

"Would you look at that?" the reporter's voice was filled with quiet awe as she looked over his shoulders.

Jamie sat on a bench, next to a young girl who must have been close to the same age. She had slipped off one tennis shoe, and handed it to the other child. Then she went to work unlacing the other shoe. The joy in her eyes as she took the battered, filthy shoes the other child wore and slipped them onto her socked feet brought tears to Matt's eyes. Sniffles surrounded him and he glanced at the news crew. There was not one dry eye among them.

"Did you get that?" the reporter asked a cameraman, who adjusted his camera so he could fish a handkerchief from his pocket. "Got it."

Mac Mahoney clapped him on the shoulder once more. "That's some girl you got there."

"Thank you, sir."

"I heard what you said to those reporters. I don't know what trouble you've got brewing that would make you pull out of the race—I was going to vote for you, by the way—but anyone in the public eye has to trust God with their kids." He pointed at Raven, who wiped her brow with the back of her hand and said something to a recipient as she dished baked beans onto his plate. Whatever she said brought a smile to the old man's face. "That one," Mac said. "She's the one I have to leave with God or I'd go crazy."

"I know how you feel." And he didn't mean father to father. "Raven drives me crazy sometimes too."

Mac chuckled. "She'll come around. God promised my children would have an inheritance in Him. All of my children. So I try not to be too pushy and just to let God work out the details behind the scenes."

"It must be difficult not to worry all the time."

Mac shook his head. "Faith in God—that's the easy part. Now, keeping my mouth shut when I want to preach at her…that's not so easy. But back to your daughter. I can see you'd like to take her and go home away from these reporters. But you can't lock her away somewhere to keep her from pricking her finger on a spinning wheel. You'll have to trust God with her. From the looks of it," he nodded toward Jamie as she laughed and talked with the child with whom she'd exchanged shoes, "she's obviously already listening to Him. So maybe you should too."

"What do you mean?"

"What might have happened if your daughter hadn't shown up today?"

"You mean other than her not being on camera?"

"That little girl would have never gotten her new shoes."

"Hundred-and-fifty-dollar shoes."

"That you can afford to replace, no sweat. That is more than most of these people make in a week."

"You're right, of course." Matthew willed his heart to stop racing, fingers of fear to stop clutching his gut in a nauseating squeeze. "We'll stay and finish the work."

"Atta boy." Mac grinned. "If we're lucky there might be a few hot dogs left at the end of the day."

"Mac, honey, there you are." A red-headed senior citizen took possession of Mac's arm. "You aren't overdoing it, are you?"

He smiled at the woman and kissed her forehead, eliciting a look of utter adoration. "I'm not overdoing it. Just watched Matt's daughter give away her shoes to another little girl."

"How precious." The woman's face glowed. She extended veiny French-manicured hands. "I'm Ruth. Mac's fiancée."

"Congratulations on your upcoming wedding. When's the happy day?"

Ruth leaned in and spoke in a conspiratorial tone. "Don't tell anyone, but we've decided to throw a real shindig at the cabin. We'll announce it during this visit and we're getting married at the family cabin during our fall get-together. Isn't that a good idea? The family all planned to be there anyway."

"I won't be." Raven's voice, rife with anger, shot forward as she approached the three of them. "Dad, this is idiotic. That woman isn't right for you."

Shock bolted through Matthew at the venomous glare she gave Ruth. "Raven?" He reached for her arm.

"Stay out of this, Matthew. It doesn't concern you."

Mac fixed Raven with a stern glare. "Raven, my girl. You're treading some bad water coming off with that attitude."

"Well, I'm sorry, but that's the best I can do."

"No, I'm sorry." Mac pulled Ruth closer. "I'm sorry that you can't accept the new love in my life. But we will be getting married in November. Now, I'd love for all of my daughters to be there, but we're getting married either way…with or without you."

Raven's gaze narrowed at the last few words. Her

eyes darted from one to the other. "Well, Dad. Denni and Keri will both be there, so apparently you'll have all your daughters at your side to celebrate the tragic event."

The frown on Mac's face mirrored Matthew's. "What are you talking about?"

Tears trailed down Raven's cheeks. "Let's face it, we both know you're not my real dad."

The man's face blanched. An obvious weakness came over him and his hand stole toward his chest. "How'd you know?"

Ruthie interjected before Raven could answer. "No. You've upset him enough. His blood pressure can't take sudden stress combined with this heat."

Mac clutched his chest and toppled. Matthew reached him just in time to soften his landing. Raven sprinted to his side.

"Dad!"

"Someone call 911," Ruth screeched.

Raven's wail reverberated off the cafeteria walls. "Daddy, I'm sorry. Don't die." She looked up at the ceiling. "God, don't let him die. Don't let him die!"

Chapter Eighteen

"Stop fussing over me," Mac groused as Ruth brought him a glass of water and fluffed his pillow.

"You heard what the doctor said." Ruth waved away his protests and fluffed all the more. "Your blood pressure shot up, you need to drink plenty of fluids and rest for a couple of days."

Raven watched from the doorway of her guest bedroom/office. Guilt plagued her that she'd been the cause of Mac's collapse. Even though the doctor had assured them that he'd passed out because of not drinking enough fluids and working too hard in the intense July heat, she couldn't squash the condemning words forming themselves in her mind. Mac could have died because of her selfishness.

She forced a smile and strode into the room. "Ruth's right, Dad. You need to let us pamper you."

Ruth stared up at her over Mac's head. The woman's pale-blue eyes softened with understanding that a truce had been declared.

"Listen, you two." Raven gathered a steadying

breath. For Dad's sake, she could do this…"I'm sorry for my outburst earlier. I'll come to the wedding."

Mac took her hand and pressed a kiss to her fingers. "That's my girl."

"Praise the Lord," Ruth said, a grin splitting her heavily made-up face. "It wouldn't have been the same without you."

"Thank you." Raven cleared her throat, uncomfortable, as always, with this sort of emotional display. "Well, I suppose I ought to…"

"You two need to talk," Ruth broke in. "I'll go see what I can rustle up for dinner."

"Do you think Dad's up to that sort of conversation?" Raven asked, peering down at Mac's pale face.

A scowl broke over his expression. "Why don't you ask me? I'm laying right here."

"Fine then, I will." Sickness had done nothing for his surliness. "Do you really think you should have an intense conversation right now? And you know it's going to be heavy duty, given the topic."

"I think it's a conversation that's way overdue."

His softened tone bespoke a contrition that went straight to Raven's heart.

"That settles it, then." Ruth headed for the door.

"Do you want me to come with you and show you where everything is?"

Ruth sent her a wink, showing way too much blue eye shadow. "Honey, if there's one thing I know, it's my way around a kitchen. I'll find what I need." She flitted out the door as though she owned the place.

Once they were alone, Mac patted the edge of the bed for Raven to sit. Quick tears rose to her eyes as he gave her a tender smile. "First, I want to say how sorry I am that you had to find out on your own. Your mother and

I always meant to tell you, but we put it off for so long, it just never seemed to matter."

"I figured it out when Mom died." Raven could barely speak around the lump in her throat. "I found my original birth certificate in some of her things."

A faraway look entered Mac's misty eyes. "We decided to hang onto it in case you ever needed to find your biological father. I wanted you to have proof."

"I met your mother while she was carrying you and I fell in love with her at first sight. I remember the first time I placed my hand on her rounded belly and felt you move inside her." His voice thickened, and he swiped at his eyes. "You were my child from that day forward."

"Then why not just put your name on my birth certificate to begin with?"

Mac released a breath. "We wanted to be honest. It was important that we start our life together in truth."

"Sounds a little idealistic to me."

He nodded. "We were young, newly married, new Christians. That was during the Jesus movement when everyone was down to basics and radical in their faith. We just wanted to do what we felt was right."

Raven couldn't keep the bitter laugh from leaving her lips. "So you put Josiah Thatcher's name on the birth certificate. How long until you adopted me?"

"A few months. We had to get the money together and go through the process."

"If you were so insistent on truth above all, why was I halfway through college and still didn't know? Didn't you think I would wonder why I looked so different from everyone in the family? I stuck out like a sore thumb."

"I always thought your looks made you stand apart like a rare and beautiful rose."

"I never felt like a beautiful rose. I remember once in biology when we were learning about the different hair colors, I learned that two redheads couldn't have a child with black hair. Later, I learned I had misunderstood, but I believed it at the time. I went to Mom and asked her if I'd been switched at birth and told her why I suspected as much."

"She never told me."

"Yeah, well," Raven said, reliving the memory of the conversation she—at fourteen years old—had had with her mother. "When I told her my theory, she laughed and said she had been dying her hair for so many years she couldn't remember what her natural color was, but she promised me that she had indeed carried me for nine and a half months, and I was without a doubt her child."

Mac looked longingly into space and emitted a short laugh. "She was miserable going so far past her due date. I think if you hadn't come when you did, she'd have threatened the doctor's life."

Raven smiled. She'd heard the same story many times. How her mother had driven over rocky roads to try to shake her labor into gear. Had walked miles on end, per the doctor's suggestion, and finally had tried relaxation techniques, which didn't work, but made her feel better while she waited the three more days it took for Raven to deign to be born. "Dad, why did the two of you decide not to tell me that I wasn't yours?"

"You *were* mine." His eyes glinted determinedly. "In every way that counted."

"I know." Raven took his hand and pressed it to her cheek. "You're my dad. And I love you. But what made you and Mom decide to keep this from me?"

He shrugged and squeezed her hand. "Denni came

along when you were still too young for us to tell you, and then Keri two years later. We just didn't want to make you feel like you were any less special to me. By the time you were old enough to understand, we just didn't think about it."

"And when Mom died? Did you think of it then?"

Pain flashed in his eyes. "That's why I need to ask your forgiveness. I was just being selfish. I didn't want anything to come between us. But something did, only I had no idea what was bothering you—that you'd found out the truth—until today."

"Maybe I should have come to you a long time ago." Raven mourned the years that she'd wasted being bitter against this wonderful man who had raised her with all the love of a natural father. "And I might not have now, except that…" She gathered a deep breath. "My biological brother has contacted me."

Mac's gaze darted to hers, instantly alert. "Really?"

She nodded. "Apparently he did it as a surprise for Josiah."

Again, pain flashed in his eyes. "I see. And did you meet Josiah before he died?"

"Oh, he's not dead. What gave you that idea?"

"He's not? Have you met him?"

"Well, not yet. Sonny wanted to meet me first and verify that I'm really biologically connected." She couldn't bring herself to say "Josiah's daughter." Not to Mac. There was no way she could bear to hurt him with those words.

"But you have met Sonny?"

Raven nodded. A sense of unease nipped at her gut. "We had dinner the other night."

"And?"

"We look alike. He gave me a photo of Josiah."

"Mind if I take a look?"

"Really? Why?"

"I have my reasons."

Raven walked to the striped chair in the corner where she'd tossed her purse when both she and Ruth had insisted upon helping him into bed. She fished her billfold out and slipped the photo Sonny had given her out of the plastic sheath.

Mac took it, studying it close. "When was the last time you spoke to this Sonny?"

Something about the way he said *this Sonny* alerted her senses. Mac had on his "cop" face. That always meant lots of questions.

"A couple of nights ago. That's when he gave me the picture."

"Raven, I don't know what this guy's game is, but I saw this picture of Josiah Thatcher in the *Kansas City Star* a few weeks ago. I recognized the name from conversations with your mother years ago, and of course as you pointed out, you're the spitting image of him."

A frown creased Raven's brow. "What was his picture doing in there?"

"Honey, it was next to his obituary."

A burst of laughter shot from Raven's lips as though Mac had made that up just to lighten the tension between them.

"I'm serious, Raven. Ask Ruth. She was there. I told her everything that day. If you've been investigating your family, why didn't you already know this, ace?"

Raven shook her head. "It's been a while. I just, I don't know. I slacked off on trying to locate him. Searching article databases and archives takes time. I've been working fifteen-hour days to get the anchor job. I dropped the ball on this, I guess." She frowned as a thought clung to her mind. "Besides, you have to be mistaken. Sonny is in the middle of working out the details right now for me to meet Josiah. If he were dead, Sonny surely wouldn't be stringing me along. That would just be sick."

"There's one way to find out. Go through the microfiche at the library and find the obituary."

Raven shoved herself up from the bed. "I can do better than that. I subscribe to the paper online. They archive several months back. I'm sure it will be there if you have the right guy." She strode across the room to her desk and booted up the computer.

She turned back to Mac while she waited for the sign-on screen. "Does it bother you that I am in contact with my brother?"

"I'd be lying if I said I wasn't a tad bit concerned." He sat up and stared at the computer screen.

"Dad, lie down. I'll read off anything I find."

"Oh, all right. But there's nothing wrong with me other than a little too much sun."

"Be that as it may, you need to do what the doctor ordered," Raven said, distractedly, as she found the Website and punched in her user name and password. "Okay, there are two matches for Josiah Thatcher. One…" Her throat thickened as she pulled up the obituary column. "Survived by one sister, Meredith Graham, and one son, Sonny Thatcher, both of Kansas City, Missouri." She turned to Mac. "It's true. He died weeks ago."

"I'm sorry, honey."

"I don't get why Sonny lied to me."

"You don't know him very well," Mac reminded in his practical tone. "There really wasn't any way of knowing whether he was on the up-and-up or not."

"True. And there were times…"

"What?"

"I don't know. I'm not always real comfortable around Sonny."

"Why is that?"

"It's nothing I can really put my finger on. Just instinct I guess."

"Think he's after money?"

Raven skimmed over the next article found under the search. "No. According to this, Josiah owned a couple of pretty swanky stables. He left them to Sonny. I'm a little confused about the aunt, as well. Sonny said I'm his only family now."

"Sounds like you need to beware of this new brother. He's not shaping up to be someone you'd want in your life."

"You got that right."

She jotted down her aunt's name.

"What are you doing?" Raven recognized the stern wariness in his tone. The one he used when he was about to forbid her to do something that in all likelihood could put her in harm's way.

"I'm going to find this Meredith Graham."

Bending over, she brushed a kiss across his forehead. "Get some rest, Dad. I love you."

"I love you too, Raven." He clutched her hand. "Please be careful. You don't know what sort of character Sonny is. Anyone who would lie about a dead father and an elderly aunt…"

"I know, and I plan to find out exactly what's he's up to."

He closed his eyes and Raven left the room.

Delicious smells assailed her nose as she stepped into the living room. The sound of Ruth's Southern voice singing old-time country gospel with the radio brought a completely unexpected rush of affection to Raven's heart. There was no time to analyze her absence of resentment. But Raven couldn't deny the lift it gave her to be free from the bitterness she'd lived with for so long.

She called her contact at the K.C.P.D. and thirty minutes later discovered that her aunt lived in a retirement community in one of the more upscale sections of town.

"Okay, this is it." She grabbed a phone book from the drawer and located the number of the retirement community. A pleasant enough voice answered on the third ring.

Raven cleared her throat. "Yes, I'm looking for a Meredith Thatcher. I believe she lives in one of your assisted living apartments."

"I'm sorry. We can't give out information about our residents."

"I understand completely," she said, keeping her tone even and friendly. "But could I give you my name and number and you could give it to her for me? Then she could call if she wants to."

"Now I never said we had a resident here by that name."

"Okay, fair enough. How about I give you my contact information, anyway? And if she's there and if she wants to call me, she can."

The woman hesitated for a moment. "Okay. You can do that."

Thirty minutes later, Raven hung up the phone after speaking with her aunt. The tearful conversation had taken Raven aback somewhat. Meredith's brother, Raven's biological father, had been only a day away from contacting her when he died. She seemed to want to say more, but suddenly clammed up. "I'd rather not speak about it over the phone."

They made plans for Raven to come for a visit the next evening.

Just before the elderly lady hung up, she had said, "I wouldn't mention this to Sonny. The boy has never been fond of me. And my guess is he had no intention of telling you or me about the other."

"I wish he'd given me the option at least."

"Nevermind regrets, honey," she'd said. "You've found me now, like the good reporter you are. Let's just keep this between us and you come tomorrow around suppertime. I'll have my girl prepare us a nice meal."

"Yes, ma'am. I'll be there."

Raven took inventory of her day tomorrow. So much for Sunday being a day of rest. First, she would keep her promise to God and attend service with Matthew. After all, Anaya's story would air tonight and then again tomorrow. Second, Keri had asked her to come down and help serve again. Most of the volunteers had been used up for the barbecue and didn't feel compelled to help out two days in a row. Raven hadn't had the heart to refuse. So she would spend her afternoon wearing plastic gloves and a hair net and dishing out lasagna and French bread.

By far, she looked forward to her evening with Meredith the most. Speaking with her aunt might give her the answers she needed in order to bring closure to this chapter of her life. Then maybe she would be ready to move forward...with Matthew.

Chapter Nineteen

Matthew slowly came to consciousness, awakened by raging pain behind his eyes. Fire scorched his throat and the achy feeling in his limbs, which earlier he'd suspected might be caused from adding two miles to his usual four-mile run, now caused him to thrash about trying to find a comfortable position.

With unaccustomed weakness, he sat up slowly and made his way to the bathroom medicine cabinet. He took some pain reliever, which scratched his throat as he swallowed. He walked close to the wall, then his dresser, holding tightly to whatever steady surface he could find as he made his way back to his bed. Shivering under the covers, he glanced at the clock on his nightstand. The glowing numbers read 3:18. Four hours before he needed to be up getting ready to pick Raven up for church. He closed his eyes, and even as he drifted into an uneasy sleep, he knew he'd never make it to service the next day.

When he finally awakened again, his mother stood over him, her brow creased with the worry reflected in her eyes. "You're burning up. I'm calling Rex."

Too weak and ill to argue, Matthew closed his eyes

and listened as she dialed their long-time friend and family doctor.

He was barely conscious of his mother's voice a moment later. "Rex is coming, darling." Something wet and cool touched his forehead and Matthew faded once more.

"Strep throat?" Raven's disappointment knew no bounds. How could Matt go and get strep when she needed to go to church and honor her part of the bargain with God? She couldn't get to the church alone. Not on time anyway. She hadn't been paying attention while driving with Matthew last Sunday morning.

"The doctor thinks that's what it is," Mrs. Strong replied over the phone. "But of course he won't know for sure until the culture comes back from the lab. And he can't even send it in until tomorrow. But he's given Matt a shot of penicillin, and expects he'll begin to get better in a day or so. In the meantime, it will be impossible for him to attend services this morning. He asked me to call you and let you know how sorry he is."

"Yes, ma'am. Will you please tell Matt I'm thinking about him and I wish him a speedy recovery?"

"That's very sweet of you. I'll let him know."

"Do you still plan to attend this morning, Mrs. Strong?"

Hesitation on the other end of the line brought a rush of heat to Raven's cheeks. Talk about your brazen self-invites.

"I'm sorry, dear. I'm afraid not. I don't want to leave Matthew while he's so very ill."

"Of course. I don't blame you." She wouldn't mind being by his side, herself.

"What about me?" Jamie's voice intruded upon the conversation, from another phone connected to the same line. "I want to go."

"Jamie Strong," Mrs. Strong said in firm admonishment. "What are you doing sneaking around and listening in on other people's phone conversations?"

"I wanted to ask Raven to take me to church anyway, since she was planning on going. Rovercomer is visiting today."

Rovercomer? Was that more churchese she'd forgotten?

"Please, Grams? If it's okay with Dad?"

An exasperated huff from Mrs. Strong pretty much answered the question.

"Do you still plan to attend, Raven?"

"Honestly, I don't see how I could pick up Jamie and get there on time."

"No, you'd have to attend the second service."

"Oh, that's right. There are two?" Raven's heart lifted at her second chance to honor her word.

"What time does the second one start?"

"Ten-forty-five, so you have plenty of time if you intend to go."

"Of course. That's wonderful, if I could just get some help in locating the church."

"I'll draw you a map. That is…unless you prefer not to take Jamie?"

"No, of course I don't mind, if Matt okays it."

An hour and a half later, the little girl was buckled up in the front passenger seat of Raven's SUV. She wore a pair of navy-blue dress slacks with a matching jacket. Cute.

"Hey, you look like a businesswoman in that suit. You making any career plans?"

"I'm going to be a missionary when I grow up. And anyone can wear suits. You don't have to be a businesswoman. You don't have to have a job, even, otherwise, they wouldn't make them in my size."

"So true," Raven drawled, taken in by the girl's spunk once more. "So what's Rovercomer?"

She shrugged. "A guy dressed in a big dog suit." She grinned and a sparkle lit her eyes. "He's really funny. He sings 'Let God arise and His enemies be splattered.' Get it? Splattered instead of scattered."

Nope. She didn't have a clue what was funny about it. "Oh, yeah."

"Anyway, he always gets songs messed up. But he doesn't get discouraged and always tries to do better because he's Rovercomer. Like overcomer only with an *r*."

"Ah, I get it." Sort of.

"So, I guess you know Dad's real sick."

"Yeah. We'll have to bring him some egg drop soup to make him feel better."

"Yeah. He loves that."

"Yeah."

Just when Raven thought they might have an entire conversation based on non sequiturs and repeated words, the pillared front of the brick church came into view.

When they entered the church, Raven stopped in the foyer before heading for the sanctuary. She turned to Jamie. "Okay, listen, meet me right here after church, okay?"

She rolled her eyes. "You have to sign me in and out or I can't go. Why do you think my dad let me come with you?"

Embarrassment shot through her. "Oh. Well, then, lead the way."

"Are you going to remember me when church is over? I don't want to be left here all alone."

"Of course I'm not going to forget about you, Jamie. I promise."

The second service couldn't have been more different from the more traditional service she'd attended the week before. Raven connected with the upbeat music, a less crowded sanctuary and a contemporary message given by the youth pastor. Her heart lifted and for the first time since her mother's death, she felt ready to trust in God again. There were no tears, no public confessions of rededication, only a simple knowing in her heart that she was forgiven and accepted back. Like the prodigal son. By the time the service ended, Raven wondered if she looked as different on the outside as she felt on the inside. She couldn't keep a cheesy grin from her face as she slid out of the pew and into the middle aisle.

"Excuse me." Raven felt a tap on her shoulder. She turned to find a thirty-something woman smiling, her plump cheeks pushed upward and her blue eyes shining with excitement.

"Can I help you?"

"Aren't you Raven Mahoney from Channel 23?"

Ha! Take that Ken! Someone finally recognized her.

"That's me." She returned the woman's smile.

"Wow. I was just wondering if anyone called about Anaya."

"Not yet. But we're still hoping."

"My children have been following the story and pray for her every night."

Raven grasped the woman's hand, fighting a sudden rush of tears. "Tell your children thank you and please to keep praying. I know for a fact that God is listening on this one."

Before she made it five more feet, someone else stopped her. And another person and another. People had seen her, not only on Channel 23, but the network story had run the night before and everyone wanted to know about little Anaya.

Jamie's scowling face greeted her when she arrived, breathless from rushing, at the Kids' Church entrance. "I'm the last one," Jamie groused. She crossed her arms over her chest while Raven signed her out. "I knew you'd forget all about me."

Jamie walked a good three feet ahead of her and kept up a quick pace, obviously trying to keep Raven from catching up. "Jamie, stop a second," she said when they got outside.

The little girl halted, but didn't turn around. With a sigh, Raven stepped in front of her, face-to-face. "No, I didn't forget you, Jamie. I kept getting stopped by people who saw the broadcast about Anaya. People are praying. Lots and lots of people." Unable to contain this newfound joy, she grabbed the little girl and hugged her tightly. "Isn't that wonderful?"

Jamie wriggled free, her face still as stone. "Yeah, that's great. Can we go now?"

"Okay, sure." Raven received the rejection with as much understanding as she could find in her heart. After all, the little girl had never indicated that she'd like to be hugged by Raven. She'd never even expressed the merest liking for her.

"Hey, Jamie?" She buckled up, and cranked the engine. "What?"

"I'm really sorry I grabbed you and hugged you like that. I was invading your personal space. I won't do it again without your permission."

Jamie gave her trademark shrug. "It's okay. But I have a mother, you know."

Ah, that explained it. "Yes, I do know. I met Casey years ago."

"When you and Dad were engaged?"

"Yes."

"Do you think you're going to marry him?"

"I don't know, Jamie."

"If you did marry him, I probably wouldn't call you Mom."

Something in the way she said *probably* gave her away. But Raven refused to call her on this one. Jamie was effectively letting her know it was okay with her if Matthew married her. That was huge. And Raven didn't take it lightly.

"I tell you what. Let's wait and see what happens before we decide what you're going to call me, okay?"

Another shrug.

Raven put the SUV in gear and headed out of the parking lot toward the freeway. Just as she pulled onto the ramp, her phone chirped from her purse.

"Hand me that, will you, James?"

"Raven, it's Keri. Where are you? I could use your help, pronto."

"I went to the late service. I'm on my way to drop off Jamie at home, then I'm headed right over."

"Okay, hurry."

Raven flipped the phone closed with one hand while keeping her focus on the emerging traffic as she passed an off ramp going sixty-five.

"Can I go with you today?" Jamie asked, taking the phone and slipping it once more into Raven's bag.

"After yesterday, I doubt your dad would let you. I noticed they used every single shot of you. By the way, did anyone mention it at Kids' Church?"

She rolled her eyes. "Just about everyone. Even Rovercomer."

Raven chuckled.

"So? Can I?"

"I don't know. We could call and ask. Use my phone."

"Thanks!"

Jamie dialed. "Grams? Raven says it's okay with her if it's okay with you if I go to the mission and help pass out food again. So can I?"

Silence invaded the vehicle while Jamie listened. "Please, Grams? I promise Raven'll take good care of me." She gave a huff. "Miss Mahoney, then."

Raven's lips twitched.

Silence. And more silence.

"Did she hang up on you?" Raven finally asked.

"She's going to ask my dad if I can go."

She perked up again. "Thanks, Grams." She handed Raven the phone. "Grams says I can go, but she wants to talk to you."

Mindful of the traffic on either side of her, Raven took the phone in her left hand so she could maneuver with her right. "Yes, Mrs. Strong?"

"Matthew has agreed to allow Jamie to help out, but he asked me to ask you to make sure you don't let her out of your sight unless she's with someone you trust implicitly."

"I promise."

"Fine. And when will you have her home?"

"Probably around four-thirty. Is that all right?"

"Yes, I suppose so. Just, please take good care of her."

Raven's heart went out to the woman. She'd essentially lost her daughter, and couldn't bear the thought of losing her granddaughter as well. "I will look after her as if she were my own."

"Thank you."

"How's Matt feeling?"

"Still very badly. The doctor said it would take at least twenty-four hours for him to feel any better. I haven't seen him this miserable since he had a bad case of the chicken pox in seventh grade. They never get too old that you don't worry about them when they're ill."

"I can imagine."

"You'll find out some day when you have children of your own."

"Yes, ma'am."

"I'll let you go. You shouldn't be driving and talking anyway. That's much too dangerous."

"I agree. I'll have your girl back in a few hours. And thanks again for letting her come."

Jamie settled back in the seat, a smile plastered on her pretty, freckled face. "It's good to help people, isn't it?"

"I think it is."

"Gramps used to say, 'Let's roll up our sleeves and do some good in this world.' That's what I liked best about him. He was always helping people."

"He was a great man."

"Yeah…"

A natural silence hung over the SUV. She understood how Jamie felt. She'd sensed that Jamie was unique in some way, but she'd had no idea just how remarkable the little girl really was. Matthew had to be so proud. And she, if given the chance to mother this little girl, would have to pray hard so she didn't mess her up.

From the recesses of the fever-induced fog, Matthew heard the chirping of his cell phone. He waited, expecting his mother to come answer it. The chirping stopped and he relaxed again. But only for a minute as the caller persisted.

Pain sliced his eyes as he lifted his head from the pillow and reached toward his nightstand where his cell phone rested in its charger. "Yes?" He whispered to save his throat the additional pain of vibrating vocal cords.

"Matthew Strong?"

"Yes."

"Are you okay, man? You sound hoarse or something."

"I'm a little sick. What can I do for you?"

"Raven Mahoney left this number as a contact in case I couldn't reach her."

"In reference to what?"

"I'm Tony from the Kansas City P.D. I was running an e-mail address for her."

"Oh, yes. What did you find out."

"Well, this guy was good. I have to say that much. He routed that one message through six different e-mail addresses, each with a different user name. Similar to the way spammers do it."

Matthew's head spun and he lay back with a groan. "Long and short of it, pal. I'm half-dead, here."

"Okay, we finally ran it back far enough to find the credit card used to pay for e-mail service. The guy's name is Sonny Thatcher. Ring a bell?"

"Not at all."

"Well, he might be working with someone else. But turns out, this guy is being investigated in another case for something completely different than e-mail threats."

"What's that?"

"I can't really give details. But he's definitely bad news."

"Well, thank you for calling. I'll let Raven know."

Wearily, he shut the phone, feeling the frustration of encountering another dead end.

Sonny Thatcher. He had no clue who that might be, nor why the man would want to take his daughter. At any rate, there was nothing he could do now…all he needed to do was get well…

To sleep…

Chapter Twenty

The Victory Mission was abuzz with activity when Raven and Jamie walked through the door. Raven recognized the news team from the day before, and the frenzied excitement as the reporter rushed forward and stuck a microphone in her face.

"Raven Mahoney, how did you feel when you heard the news?"

She frowned, trying to wrap her mind around why the news team would be back so soon, and for crying out loud, would this woman move out of her personal space?

"I wish I knew what you were talking about," she muttered, glancing about, using old reporter tactics of taking in her surroundings. "Noticing the small things," as Jonesy used to say.

Her heart thundered in her ears as she spied a beaming couple in the corner, fawning over a child—Anaya. Her mind connected with the image and she smiled.

"I'm so glad you're finally here!" Keri pulled her away from the reporter, who didn't bother taking the hint and followed as the two sisters headed toward the reunion.

"Kere, is this what I think it is?" she asked breathlessly.

Keri's mass of unruly red curls bounced with her vigorous nod. "Anaya has a family, Rave."

"After one broadcast?"

"Yes! Can you believe it?"

Keri stopped before a gray-haired woman who held Anaya tightly in her ample brown arms.

"Mrs. Ford, I'd like to introduce you to my sister, Raven Mahoney."

The woman's eyes filled with tears. She grabbed hold of Raven with one arm, keeping a firm hold on Anaya with the other. "I don't know how to thank you for working so hard to find us."

"I'm speechless." And she truly was. How on earth had this happened so quickly?

She turned to Keri, who seemed to read her thoughts. "Mr. and Mrs. Ford recognized Mary's picture. They called as soon as the number flashed across the screen during the six o'clock news last night. They were on a plane first thing this morning."

"Why didn't you call me?"

"I wanted you to be surprised. That's why I took a chance you might volunteer today, even though just two weeks ago you'd have blown me off like a bottle of bubbles."

"Consider it the new me." Raven's lips twisted into a wry grin.

"That's what I was counting on."

"You mean we're not going to help serve lunch?"

At the sound of Jamie's disappointed voice, Raven came to attention. Good grief. She'd already forgotten about the kid. Some mother she would make!

Justin stepped up and placed his hand on the girl's shoulder. "Of course you are. Come with me. We'll get you some plastic gloves and you can hand out dinner rolls."

Jamie's countenance exploded with happiness. Raven started to follow, but the reporter from the network caught hold of her. "Wait, we'd like to film you and ask some questions."

"I'm sorry." Raven pulled away so that the woman's hand slipped away from her. "This is about Anaya and her grandparents."

"My boss would like me to interview you." She gave her a pointed look. "In-ter-view."

Understanding dawned. They wanted her on air, and would possibly hire her. It was what she'd always wanted. To advance to a national network. But as she watched Jamie walk away, chatting happily with Justin, she knew where she needed to be. She looked back to the reporter and shrugged. "Sorry. I have to stay with that little girl and make sure she's safe."

Keri squeezed her hand. "Good choice," she whispered.

Contentment stole over Raven. She pressed a quick kiss to Anaya's beautiful face and offered Mr. Ford her hand. "Congratulations on finding your grandbaby, Mr. and Mrs. Ford."

"Without you, this never would have happened."

Raven shook her head. "God gets all the credit for this one."

"Praise the Lord," Mrs. Ford exulted.

The reporter turned away from Mrs. Ford and rolled her eyes, but Raven caught a glimpse of the sneer on her lips. A sneer that reminded Raven of her own attitude a mere two weeks earlier.

"Amazing how quickly one's perspective can change, isn't it?" Keri broke into her thoughts as they walked away.

"You saw her look too?"

Keri nodded. "Now you understand how I could so easily give up my chance to be Briarwood's first female chief of police. I just had better things to do."

Arm-in-arm, they walked into the serving area. Relief flooded the volunteers' faces. A sixty-something woman wearing a hairnet and plastic gloves replaced a pan of rolls into the serving dish and nodded toward them. "I hope you two are ready to help. That hooplah in there with the little girl and the media has drawn so much attention, we're swarmed with people wanting to eat. We're almost as busy as Thanksgiving and Christmas."

"I'm sorry, Sharon," Keri said, to the frustrated volunteer. "Tell us what we can do to help."

Sharon motioned toward a small table at the end of the serving line. "Drinks cups need to be filled and another couple of tea urns will need to be filled. But you'll have to brew it."

Raven leapt into action and began filling disposable cups with ice cubes and tea. Thirty minutes later, she headed to the kitchen to brew some more, per Sharon's instructions.

Justin stood over an oven, lifting a pan of lasagna from the four-hundred-degree furnace.

Raven glanced about as she headed for the sink. She frowned and her gut tightened. "Where's Jamie?"

Justin set the pan on the stainless-steel countertop. He glanced about, a frown creasing his brow. "She was just here a little bit ago, I had her putting rolls on the pans to go in the oven.

Raven followed his gaze to the empty floor space in front of two large pans filled with brown-and-serve dinner rolls.

"Justin!" Raven's panicked voice echoed through the kitchen. "Where is she?"

The kitchen door swung open and Keri rushed in. "What's wrong?"

"Jamie's gone!" Raven's panicked screech shot through the air like an arrow.

"Raven, calm down. We'll find her." Keri's voice remained low and even. "She's probably just in the bathroom."

Gathering in a deep breath, Raven nodded. "I'll go check."

"I'm coming with you." Keri stayed planted to her side. "I'm sure she's just making a pit stop." But all three bathrooms were empty.

Raven's heart raced a hundred miles a second. Not again. If she didn't find Jamie soon, she knew it would explode inside her chest. "I know exactly how Mary must have felt on the road from Jerusalem when Jesus was twelve and went missing. She eventually found him in the temple."

Raven's eyes grew wide and she and Keri exchanged glances. "The chapel," they said in unison.

"Do you really think?" Raven's dress shoes clicked on the hard floor with every step.

"We'll find out." Keri opened the door.

"Jamie!" Raven rushed forward. Jamie sat on the front row of chairs with a man wearing army surplus. His stench nearly bowled Raven over as she approached. It was one thing for Jamie to serve in public where she could be watched, where no one could hurt her or whisk her away. Another thing altogether, for her to be alone in a closed room with a man who could be anything.

"Hey, Raven." Jamie glanced up. "This is Ray. He likes the Cardinals too."

An eerie recognition began to play at the corners of Raven's mind. She searched her memory until she found his face. The video footage from last Sunday. This was the man extorting money from the Strongs. The man who had beaten Casey so badly she could no longer function beyond childhood levels.

Jamie's natural father.

Cold waves of fear slid up her spine. "Keri, please take Jamie to the kitchen for me," she said, her tone deadly still, calm.

"Hey, I'm talking to Ray." Jamie's outrage shook in her voice.

"Jamie, you promised to stay where I could keep an eye on you. You broke that promise by leaving the kitchen. Now, please stop mouthing off and go with Keri like I said."

Whether she was shocked into submission, or afraid Raven would rat her out to Matt, Jamie did as she was told without another word of protest.

The man stared her down, silently. He didn't move to run away. He didn't defend himself. Neither spoke until Keri and Jamie were out of the room.

"You're a hard man to find, Ray."

"Obviously not. You're looking at me."

"Yes, and you're going to be looking at the inside of a jail cell in a few short minutes."

"You can't arrest someone for sitting in a chapel talking to a little girl."

"How about attempted kidnapping, threatening letters and e-mails? Those are strong enough reasons, don't you think?"

Ray frowned and fear flickered in his eyes. "I told you, we were just sitting here talking. I wasn't going to kidnap her. That thought never even crossed my mind. And I'm not sure what you're getting at with the threatening letters and e-mails, but do you really think I own a computer?"

Logic never failed to hit its mark with Raven and she allowed her thought processes to go to bat for her. If Ray had been the man who'd attempted to kidnap her, wouldn't Jamie have recognized him now? Even if he'd been disguised that day at Adventure Park, there should have been something about him to tip her off.

"Matt thinks it was you."

"Me what?" He studied her. "Did someone try to kidnap my daughter?"

"Okay, first of all, she's not your daughter. You gave up that right. Second of all, I'm not discussing this with you. You'll have to discuss it with the police."

"I didn't do anything."

"I happen to know you violated the terms of your parole by not showing up for a drug test."

"That was a misunderstanding of the date. And I got it all worked out. Call my parole officer, if you don't believe me."

Raven didn't want to believe him. She just wanted the threats to end, for Jamie to be safe, for Matt to rest easy knowing everything was okay. "Why should I listen to a man who extorted money from the family whose daughter he victimized?"

He dropped to a chair and buried his face in his hands. "I know you're right. I'm not the same man I was a few weeks ago. I've been staying at the men's shelter a few blocks from here. It's a lot like this one, only just for men. The only way you can stay there is if you attend nightly church services. At first I went to the services just so I could have a cot to sleep on. Then I started listening and I got saved."

"Oh, come on." Raven gave an exasperated sigh. "I should have known you'd play the 'God changed me' card."

"But He did." Ray looked up. "Don't you think some-one like me can get help from God? I haven't had a drop to drink or any drugs in a month."

"What were you doing here?"

"Part of our recovery is staying caught up on current events. We watch the nightly news." He nodded toward the door Jamie had slipped through. "I saw her giving that little girl her shoes."

"So you saw her on the news. How'd you know it was her?"

"They showed a clip with Matthew in it. Jamie looks just like me. I put two and two together. I might be poor and a recovering addict, but I'm pretty smart. When I heard the news trucks were back, I thought she might be here. I just wanted to see her in person."

"One more thing. What makes you think you had a right to pull Jamie aside and talk to her?"

"I didn't. I didn't even plan it. I was in the chapel and she walked in. Said God wanted her to pray for me."

Taken aback, Raven wasn't sure how to respond. She gaped.

Ray nodded. "I know. I didn't know what to say either. But I didn't have to say anything, because she did the talking. Prayed for me to be strong and good. And that God would help me to find a place to live and a job so I could take care of myself." He shook his head as though still in disbelief himself. "Funny thing is, I had just been praying those exact things when she walked in."

"Okay. So you honestly haven't been harassing Matt?"

"Nope. I probably would have gone back to him and tried for more cash if I was still using, but not now."

"Would you be willing to tell him face-to-face?"

He shrugged. "I guess."

"All right. Hang on a sec."

Raven dialed Matthew's cell.

After a few rings, his voice mail picked it up. Raven disconnected and dialed the main line. His mother answered.

"Mrs. Strong, this is Raven."

"Is everything all right with Jamie?"

"Yes. She's fine. I need to speak with Matthew. It's urgent."

"I'm sorry, Raven, Matthew's out like a light. The doctor gave him a prescription-strength pain reliever for his throat and he's been asleep now for two hours. I doubt I could wake him if I tried."

Disappointment clutched at Raven. She was so ready to get this chapter of Matt's life closed for him. "All right. Will you please give him a message to call me just as soon as he wakes up? As I said, it's urgent."

"I hope nothing is wrong."

"I wish I could tell you, Mrs. Strong, but I'm not at liberty to share this with anyone but your son. I'll let Matthew fill you in later."

"I understand."

She hung up and focused her gaze once more on Ray. "Matthew's too ill to talk. Do you have the number for the other mission?"

Ray reached into his grimy pocket and pulled out a card. Raven fought to keep her disgust to herself as she took the filthy thing and dialed the number.

"Gospel Mission."

"Yes, I'd like to confirm that you've had a certain resident there working your drug and alcohol program."

"I'm sorry, we don't give out information over the phone."

"Look, he's sitting here in front of me and told me he's been down there. I'm at the Victory Mission a few blocks away from you. My sister and her husband are administrators of the place."

"Justin and Keri?"

"Yes, I'm Raven Mahoney. Keri's sister."

"The reporter?"

Someone else who recognized her. Strangely, the sense of satisfaction she'd once had was missing. "Yes."

"May I speak with the resident in question?"

She handed her phone to Ray, fighting harder than ever not to wince as he put it up to his ear.

"This is Ray Marx. That you, Alan?"

After a minute of conversation, Ray handed the phone back. She had no choice but to swallow down her revulsion and hope no bugs had crawled out of his hair and onto her phone. Why didn't these places insist upon showers?

"This is Raven."

"All right. I can confirm that Ray has been a resident here for the past few weeks. As far as I know he has not had a drop of alcohol or any drugs during that time, but we don't force them to stay in house. He's met with his parole officer on a weekly basis and has passed each drug screening with flying colors. He's about to move into the next phase of the program where we teach about personal hygiene and social interaction."

That's a mercy.

Raven thanked him and closed her phone to disconnect the call.

"So your story pans out. You going to be there when Matt's well enough to check out your newly turned-over leaf?"

"I'll be there."

"One more thing, Ray. Jamie's off limits."

He gave a sad nod. "I know."

Raven watched him shuffle out of the chapel. Realization struck her that she might very well have lost Jamie today—for the second time. She glanced at her watch. Still a little earlier than she'd told Mrs. Strong she'd have Jamie back, but the weight of responsibility hung over her like an anvil. She couldn't bear the thought of being the one to lose Matthew's most precious treasure.

Amid protests from the willful little girl, Raven loaded her into the car and drove her home. When they pulled into the circular drive, she walked to the door with a silent, brooding Jamie.

Not quite as angelic as the temperament she'd displayed at the mission.

Mrs. Strong seemed relieved that they'd arrived home safely. She hugged Jamie close and then kept a protective arm around the child's shoulders as she faced Raven.

"How is Matt?" Raven asked.

"Still sleeping. I felt his brow a little while ago and he seems to be a bit cooler than before, though still feverish to the touch."

"Please give him my best and ask him to call me as soon as he's well enough to talk."

Mrs. Strong's countenance softened. "Would you like to come into the kitchen for tea or coffee?"

Raven smiled, warmed by the invitation and aware that the woman was indeed extending a welcome back into Matthew's life. "I appreciate the offer a great deal. But I have a dinner appointment. And I want to check on my dad before I head that way."

The warmth left Mrs. Strong's face and in its place a suspicious frown appeared. "A dinner appointment?"

A wry grin tipped Raven's lips. She really couldn't blame the woman. Not considering their past. "With my aunt."

"I see."

"But I'll have my cell phone on and handy, so as soon as Matt's up to it, I'll take his call."

"All right. And thank you for taking Jamie with you today."

"It was my pleasure. She's truly an inspiration at the mission."

Jamie gave a very uninspiring scowl. "I'd like to go up to my room, Grams."

"All right, but don't bother your dad."

"I won't."

Mrs. Strong turned back to Raven, a questioning frown creasing her brow.

"She's a little upset that we had to leave earlier than planned."

"She's a willful child. Stubborn, like Matthew. But I expect you'll be able to handle it."

Raven's brow rose as surprise shot through her.

"You love my son. This time, I doubt you'd have the heart to let him go."

"You're right."

"Jamie comes with the deal."

"I know. And I wouldn't have it any other way."

Mrs. Strong stepped forward and gave Raven a quick hug. "I hope you'll come to dinner as soon as Matthew is on his feet again."

"Thank you. I'd love it."

Raven's mind buzzed as she drove away. After a long fifteen years of bitterness, secrets and the pain of loneliness, she felt as thought she'd walked into a burst of sunshine. To have Matthew back in her life, to be trusting God once more, being open with Mac about knowing that she wasn't his biological child…the truth really did make one free.

Now there were only a few unanswered questions left. And in just a couple of hours she'd know everything she needed to know.

Chapter Twenty-One

Matthew woke with a sense that something was horribly wrong.

Jamie!

"Mom!"

He sat up, dodging the pain in his skull by closing his eyes tightly. He stumbled to the door and into the hallway. "Mom!"

The ground wobbled before him, and he grappled for the wall in order to stay upright.

"Matthew!"

Relief flowed through him at the sound of his mother's voice. She took hold of his arm. "What are you doing up?"

"Is everything all right? Where's Jamie?"

"Jamie's in the kitchen having her supper. Raven brought her home a few hours ago."

"Must be the fever," he mumbled. He leaned heavily on his mother as he headed back toward his bed. "It felt like something was wrong."

"Well, everything is just fine. You go back to bed and sleep this thing off. Maybe you'll feel better tomorrow."

"Mmm..." Matthew drifted to sleep once more.

* * *

Raven stared at the forty-year-old photograph. Except for the set of the other woman's eyes, it could have been Raven herself staring back from the image.

"Startling isn't it?"

Raven looked up and shook her head at Meredith, who sat in an overstuffed rocking chair across from Raven's place on the couch. "It's uncanny. And this is you?"

The elderly woman's eyes danced. "It certainly is. I had no idea we would resemble each other so."

"Except for the eyes."

"Yes," she agreed softly. "You have your mother's eyes."

"You knew my mother?"

"Yes. Josiah brought her to my house often for dinner. I thought a great deal of her."

"I didn't realize they had a real relationship. I thought it must have been one of those sixties free-love things. A one-night-stand."

"Oh, no. They were in love. Deeply."

"What happened between them? Why would she leave when she was pregnant with me?"

Meredith's expression became one of sad remembrance. "She found out he was married. To Sonny's mother."

Raven gasped at the knowledge. "I just assumed they had met after Sonny's mother left."

"No. When your mother told Josiah she was pregnant, he confessed to having a wife. She was heartbroken. Bad enough that she'd betrayed her principles and slept with a man before marriage, but to learn she was an adulteress as well was mortifying to her."

Raven shuddered to hear her beloved mother described in such a manner. She wanted to scream at the old woman, wanted to protest. But she saw the truth written plainly on her newfound aunt's sweet face. "What happened?"

"Josiah knew he would have to choose between the two women. On the one hand, he had a son he loved, a wife who, though crazy by all accounts, was still his wife. In and out of institutions, cruel to Sonny, Josiah wouldn't have stayed as long as he did if not for Sonny. But when it came down to having to choose, he knew he couldn't let your mother walk out of his life. He begged her to give him a few days to sort things out. When he went home, he told his wife everything and asked for a divorce. Instead, she left that night and never returned."

"I can only imagine how that affected Sonny."

Meredith nodded. "He was always an odd boy. I suspect living in such a volatile atmosphere with his mom during his formative years took its toll. But once she left, it was worse. He just grew stranger and stranger. By the time he reached his teen years, I was, quite frankly, afraid to be alone with him."

"Really?" Raven's mind shifted to the times she'd felt a twinge of reservation.

"I hesitate to speak ill of anyone, but I believe the mental problems his mother suffered from were passed down to Sonny."

"Why do you think he would lead me to believe his father was alive?"

"I don't know, but I can tell you that Sonny and Josiah were not getting along very well at the end."

"Why's that?"

"Sonny discovered Josiah was looking for you and was ready to contact you. He was jealous, I suppose."

"If Sonny was so jealous, why on earth would he look me up himself?"

"I can't say. He's a strange man." The old woman stifled a yawn with the back of her hand. "Mercy."

Raven shoved herself up from the couch and grabbed her purse from the coffee table. "I'm sorry, Meredith. It's getting late. I stayed much too long."

Meredith struggled to her feet. "Nonsense. I enjoyed having you." Her watery eyes shone with sincerity as she placed a weathered hand on each of Raven's arms and held her at arm's length. "I hope you will return soon and visit me again."

"You can count on it." Raven gently pulled the old woman close.

They walked together to the door. Raven gave her one more hug before stepping onto the porch.

"I wish I could walk you all the way to your car to make sure you're all right. But I don't get around too well anymore."

"Don't worry about me. I'll be fine. And if I get nervous, I always have my cell phone handy."

Anger shot through him… Betrayed. Once again by a member of his own family. Raven was supposed to be his. Oh, he could guess the lies Aunt Meredith had spread. Now, Raven wouldn't love him. Wouldn't believe him.

The pain knifed through his heart, screaming with each agonizing slice. *I told you, Sonny. No one cares about you. No one loves you. You thought Raven would never betray you, but look…she went behind your back to find Aunt Meredith. Why didn't she tell you? Now she knows about Dad. She knows you lied. She'll never love you now. Never.*

* * *

Raven dialed home as she left the parking lot. Ruth's Texas drawl greeted her.

"Hey, Ruth. How's Dad?"

"Oh, he's growly as an ol' bear. Thinks he ought to be up and about."

"Good. Then he's feeling better."

"Do you want to talk to him?"

"No. I'll be home in about twenty minutes. I can talk to him then."

A beep on the line alerted her to a new caller. "Ruth I have another call so I'll let you go."

She said goodbye and clicked over.

"Hello?"

"Hey, sis!"

Raven's gut tightened at the sound of Sonny's cheerful voice. "How are you, Sonny?"

"Great. Want to have dinner?"

"Tonight?"

"Sure. Or have you already eaten?"

"Yes, I'm afraid I have."

"Oh? Who with?"

Raven hesitated. "Family."

"Family, huh?"

"Yeah, my Dad and his fiancée are here from out of town." Not a lie, but not forthcoming either. Meredith was already afraid of Sonny. Raven couldn't take a chance that he might confront her.

"Hey, that's great. When are you going to introduce us?"

Yeah, right, buddy.

"Maybe when you introduce me to your dad." She kept her voice light, but anger tightened her throat and she wasn't positive how convincing she sounded.

"Yes. It's definitely time for you to meet Dad. How about tomorrow night?"

Raven drew in a quick breath. "You're going to introduce us?"

"Yes. I've come to know and love you. Dad will too."

Okay, so he was obviously playing her. But Raven needed to know what he had up his sleeve. *Exactly what sort of game are you playing here, Sonny boy?*

"All right. What time then?"

"I'll pick you up from your house at say…eight?"

"My house?" Okay, she wasn't sure she wanted Sonny knowing where she lived.

"Sure. And don't worry, I already have the address."

Lord, does he seem to be threatening me?

"I can't at eight, Sonny. I have to work. They're introducing me as the new anchor tomorrow night."

"Okay. Then what time are you off?"

"I should leave the station about eleven. I'll be home by twelve."

"Midnight? That's perfect. I'll pick you up then."

Plan B started to form in her mind. No way was she getting into a car with this nutcase. Brother or no.

Raven was very glad Mac and Ruth were planning to stay a couple of more days. "Your dad will be up for visitors that late?"

"Believe me, to Dad it doesn't matter what time we come."

An uneasy shiver crawled up her spine as she said goodbye and set the phone in the seat next to her. She hit the automatic lock, hating that she was suddenly afraid of being alone in her own car.

Sonny pulled alongside the curb halfway down the block from Raven's house and watched her pull into her driveway. Night-vision goggles provided him an adequate view.

He could have taken care of things tonight. But how much more fun to make her squirm. By now she was aware that his dad was dead. But she didn't know he knew she knew. That was what made tonight so sweet. Her mind would concoct a thousand different questions. Different scenarios. He watched her until she closed the door and the front light went black.

He reached over and patted the tattered stuffed cat. Tomorrow…

Mac was sitting up waiting when Raven walked inside. Her heart rate slowed to a steady beat as she relaxed, knowing she was safe. She hadn't realized how lonely the nights were, coming home to an empty house, now even emptier since her childhood toy had gone missing.

"Hi, Dad. What are you still doing up?"

"You know I can't sleep until you're home, safe and sound."

Raven tossed her keys on the counter and walked into the living room. She flopped down beside Mac on the sofa and curled her legs up under her. "I'm a big girl, now. I can take care of myself." She hoped. "But it's nice to have you here, just the same."

"I'm worried about you, Raven. What did the aunt have to say?"

"She told me some things about how Mom and Josiah parted ways. He was married. She didn't know. That kind of stuff."

Dad nodded. "I met your Mom three weeks after their breakup. She came to Briarwood for a new start. Just sort of started driving and stopped in Briarwood. I was a new deputy back then, and found her sleeping in her car in the park."

"Dad! You didn't arrest her, did you?" Raven grinned. She knew this story by heart. She hadn't known the details leading up to Mom's arrival in Briarwood, but their meeting had always tweaked her sense of romance.

Tomorrow was so uncertain. What would she do if Sonny gained an upper hand? If his intentions were sinister somehow? This sort of felt like the calm before her storm. A sigh left Raven and she leaned against Mac, resting her head on his shoulder.

He reached up and patted her head. "*She* arrested *me*. My heart anyway. I saw her curled up in the seat, sleeping like a baby. She was just so beautiful." He expelled a nostalgic sigh. "I took her over to the diner, bought her breakfast and Dottie hired her on the spot."

"And then you guys got married and that was that." Raven lifted her head and looked up at Mac. "Do you still love her? I mean, now that you're marrying Ruth?"

"Oh, hon. My heart is always going to hold a special place for your mother. She was the love of my youth. My Ruthie is a gift from God. And I love her too. In many of the same ways, but different. More settled."

"She really makes you happy, huh?"

He winked. "She does."

"Then how come you've made her wait so long?"

"I don't know. Cold feet, maybe. Or maybe I just didn't want to do something to cause more distance between you and me."

"So what changed your mind and made you decide to marry her in spite of me?"

"Ruth got fed up and threatened to move back to Texas." He grinned. "She's one feisty woman."

"Well, good for her."

"So, what about you and Matt? Things seem to be moving right along."

"Yes, I suppose they are. He still has my engagement ring."

"Ah, so he's proposed again?"

"No. He said he did that once. The offer's still on the table, but I have to go to him this time."

"Sounds like he knows what he wants."

Raven held out her left hand and stared at her bare ring finger. "So do I, Dad."

"And?"

"And I plan to do whatever it takes to get my ring back on my finger. So get ready to walk another girl down the aisle."

"I count it the greatest joy to see my firstborn married to the man God created for her."

"You really think so? I mean…what if he was supposed to be for someone else and Mom and Josiah made me by mistake? I wasn't exactly planned, you know. What if some other woman is out there who would be better for him and who would have found her way to Matt if I hadn't been around?"

Mac clutched her tightly to him. "Raven Mahoney, God makes no mistakes. No matter the details of your conception, you are a valuable part of God's plan for this world. You're irreplaceable. And there is no one better for Matthew Strong than you are."

"Thank you, Daddy. I just needed to hear you say it."

Mac placed a gentle kiss on Raven's head. She closed her eyes. For a little while she was able to dismiss all worry about meeting with Sonny tomorrow night.

Oh, Matt, I hope you're better by tomorrow. I'm finally ready to commit to you once and for all.

First, she had to settle things with her half brother.

Chapter Twenty-Two

Pent-up energy buzzed through Raven as she sat behind the anchor desk for the first time as the rightful occupant of that chair.

Two minutes to air time and she fussed with the papers on her desk, smoothed down her seafoam suit jacket. She caught a glimpse of herself on the monitor and nearly passed out. Seafoam made her look like a Martian. Why on earth hadn't she gone with a nice tan color, or basic black?

Panic began to form a ball of despair at the base of her throat. Horror of horrors, she began to cough.

Water. She needed water.

Eyes wide, she glanced around. Where was her water?

Someone cleared his throat. Loudly. She followed the direction of the sound and located Ken. He pointed to her desk. Ah. Her water. On the shelf under the desk. She sipped it gratefully and swallowed down the lump just as the assistant gave her the five…four…three…two…one…

Matthew couldn't have been more proud as he watched Raven handle her first night as anchor. She looked good. Confident. The jacket she wore gave an olive tone to her complexion, making her appear even more exotic than usual. His heart picked up a beat at the sight of her. After several days without seeing her, he was beginning to feel like the barren earth during a drought. He needed to see her again, to hold her.

A tap at the door broke his focus. "Come in."

His mother maneuvered a tray and walked across the room to his bedside.

"Mother, I could have gotten the door."

"Nonsense. You need to stay in bed covered up."

"I'm feeling a lot better. Still a little weak, but the penicillin must have finally kicked in."

"Well, here's your supper. I made chicken noodle soup. From scratch."

She lifted the lid off the silver serving bowl. Steam rose, and the aroma of garlic, onion and chicken broth tempted his stomach.

"Mmm. Smells great, Mom. Thanks."

His mother smiled broadly, proudly. She was in her element with someone to care for. "Here, turn off the TV and eat while it's hot."

"No, wait."

His mother glanced at the TV. A smile of understanding lit her eyes. "Quite the little news reporter, isn't she?"

"Yes. This is her first night as anchor. I wanted to tape it for her just in case she wants to have it someday."

"How sweet of you. I'm sure Raven will appreciate the thought."

He shrugged and gave a little chuckle. "It probably won't matter. I imagine every member of her family is recording it as we speak."

"Speaking of Raven, she called several times yesterday to check on you."

Matthew smiled, feeling the warmth of contentment to know she cared. "I'll call her when the news is over."

"Actually, you do need to. She said there is an urgent matter she needs to discuss with you."

"When was this?"

"Yesterday."

"Mother, it's after six o'clock. Why didn't you tell me earlier?"

Her chin lifted stubbornly. "You were in no condition to worry about anything but getting better." Her silky brows rose. "And now you're better. So I was right."

"All right. I know you're worried about my getting well. But if Raven needs me, I want to get the message immediately from now on. She wouldn't say something is urgent unless it truly is."

Mother sniffed. "Fine. Next time, I'll wake you up from your sick bed. But you were so ill at the time, you wouldn't have known your own name, let alone been able to help her with her *urgent* matter."

"Mother, it's not that I don't appreciate that you've been taking care of me. But some things are not for you to decide. And anything where Raven is concerned is my business."

"Oh, fine. I suppose I'll have to get used to it. Unless I miss my guess—and you know I never do—you and Raven Mahoney will be married before the end of the year."

Matthew winked and gave her a wry grin. "If I have my way about it, we'll be married before the end of the summer. I think I've waited long enough for Raven to be my wife."

She pressed a motherly kiss to his forehead. "Good, no fever. I'll leave you to your phone call, but please do eat first so your supper doesn't get cold."

"I will."

He ate hungrily while watching the rest of the newscast. He waited until the news faded and reruns of an eighties sitcom filled the screen before he finally grabbed his cell from the nightstand and dialed her cell phone. Voice mail picked up. She most likely had the ringer set to vibrate or silent. On impulse he hung up and dialed her number at the station. Her assistant answered.

"Hello, may I speak to Raven Mahoney, please?"

"May I ask who's calling?"

"Matthew Strong."

"I'm sorry, Mr. Strong. Miss Mahoney is in a meeting and can't be disturbed."

Disappointment sifted through him. "All right. Can you tell her I called?"

After receiving her assurance, he hung up the phone and leaned back against his plumped pillow. He closed his eyes and relaxed the tension in his head.

Raven's stomach growled as she wrapped up the ten o'clock news and removed her earpiece. The planning meeting had lasted for three hours, and no one had thought to bring in any food. Now she was grouchy, hungry and more than a little nervous about her meeting with Sonny. What sort of sick game was her half brother playing by pretending their biological father was still alive?

Shaking her head in frustration, Raven felt inside her jacket pocket for her cell phone. She had only one missed call...from Matthew, but no messages. Disappointed, she slipped it back into her pocket and snatched her purse from her office before heading to the door.

She glanced around for Ken, hoping to walk to the parking lot with him, but when she located him sharing a moment of laughter with Kellie, she changed her mind. A two-minute walk to her SUV and she'd be fine. But her overactive imagination and the memory of her last conversation with her weirdo half brother made the two-minute walk seem like an eternity. She nearly fainted in relief when her SUV came into view. Her footsteps quickened on the concrete, creating an eerie resonance she could definitely live without. She beeped her car locks and reached for the door handle.

"Where you going, little sister?"

Raven screeched and jumped back as Sonny appeared next to her like something out of a nightmare. "S-Sonny," she said, trying to find the presence of mind to remain calm. "You nearly scared the life out of me sneaking up like that."

He gave a sideways grin. "Wouldn't want to scare the life out of you, would I?"

"I'd certainly hope not." *Oh, Lord, why couldn't You have made me a better actress?* "What are you doing here, anyway? I thought you were going to pick me up at my house at midnight."

"You have company."

"Yeah, my dad and his fiancée are staying with me for a few days."

"Your dad?" He frowned. "He's not your dad. My father is…"

"Well, biologically, yeah, but Mac raised me as his own. In all the ways that matter, he's my dad."

Raven knew as soon as she spoke that she'd made a mistake. Sonny's lips turned downward. "So what does that make me to you? Nothing?" He curled his long fingers around her upper arm, gouging the soft flesh with nails abnormally long for a man. "Come on." He pulled her with him as they walked further into the parking garage.

"Sonny, that hurts." She kept her tone even, praying for the presence of mind to undo the damage she'd just done. And to find a chance to make a break for it.

"You think that hurts?" He moved in close, his face inches from hers, breath reeking of alcohol and cigarettes. "You know what really hurts, Raven?"

She shook her head.

"Knowing that your father loved his cheap piece of trash's offspring more than he loved his own son. What do you think of that?"

"I don't like that you're referring to my mother in that manner."

He jerked her to a stop beside a blue beater of a car. Now it was starting to make sense. "This is your car?"

"Yeah, some reporter you are. I've been following you for weeks."

"I know, I've seen it. I saw it at home in Briarwood, I saw it on the road to St. Louis. You were following us?"

He opened the passenger-side door. "Get in."

"I don't think so." Raven stared him down. "You need help, Sonny. I don't know what you think you have planned for me, but there's no way you're getting me in that car."

His gaze narrowed and he reached around to the back of his jeans. In half a second, Raven was staring down the barrel of a .357 magnum. "Still think there's no way I'm getting you in the car?"

Well, that was one way. "All right."

"Buckle your seatbelt and don't try anything while I go around to the other side."

Sonny closed the door. Raven pulled on the belt and as she did so felt her cell bulge in her pocket. Hope sparked an idea and she plunged her hand inside, sending quick thanks to God that she'd put Matt's cell on speed dial. She felt around until she found the middle key and prayed for all she was worth that she'd found the right one. She pressed the button.

Matthew woke to the sound of his cell phone ringing on the pillow next to him.

Raven. He'd all but given up on her.

"Hello?"

The muffled sound of background noise greeted him. He glanced at the screen again. Caller ID definitely showed Raven's cell. He laughed to himself. She must have hit a wrong button and dialed him by mistake.

"Raven!" he called. "I'm on the phone here."

"What was that?" a man's voice growled.

"What was what?" That was definitely Raven's voice.

"I heard something."

"I didn't hear anything."

"Give me your purse."

"What for? Do you need money?"

Lord, is she being robbed? Matthew hit the speaker phone and sprang into action, careful not to make any noise while he dressed.

"Where's your cell phone? I know you never go anywhere without it."

"Sonny, it's not in there. Would you relax before you end up wrecking this car? You'd hate to do that, wouldn't you? These blue Pontiac Sunfires are hard to find these days. What is this, ten years old at least?"

"Your reporter mind," the man said in disgust. "Always wanting details. Well, details aren't going to help you where you're going."

Cold fear snaked down Matthew's spine. Raven was in real trouble. *Does the name Sonny Thatcher ring a bell?* Where had he heard that? His fuzzy mind recalled the earlier phone conversation. It had to be too much of a coincidence that a Sonny was out to kidnap Jamie and Raven. How could he have been so shortsighted? All along, Raven had been the one in danger. Thankfully, she'd had the presence of mind to dial his number and somehow hide her phone. *Keep the clues coming, Raven. Blue Pontiac Sunfire. Sonny.*

"All right, baby," he whispered as he grabbed the phone and headed downstairs. "Lead me to you."

"Where are we going, Sonny?" Raven's voice remained calm and clear as though she were enunciating more carefully than usual. "I know we're not going to meet your dad. I found out he's dead. Even read his obituary."

"Why do you keep calling him my dad? He's *our* dad. Only *you* shouldn't even be here."

Sonny was Raven's brother?

"You're right, of course. Mac was great to me, but I always knew I wasn't like the rest of my family. I grew up with two sisters, did I tell you that?"

"Yeah."

Good, Raven, good. Keep him talking.

Matt ran out to the car. He muffled the mouthpiece with his shirt while he cranked the engine and put it into gear.

"I used to dream about having a big brother."

"Sure you did."

"No, really. I did. That's why I was so happy when you called me. Of course I didn't know that just a couple of weeks later, you'd be kidnapping me from work and waving a gun in my face."

Given this new information, Matt drove toward the station. It was the best he could do. I need more information, Raven, honey.

"Look, Sonny. I have to use the restroom."

"Tough."

"I mean it. It's an emergency. How about stopping at that Burger King up there on the corner of Fremont and Chesterville?"

Yes! Good girl, honey.

As much as he hated to, Matt knew he had no choice but to put this call on hold and dial 911.

"Nine-one-one emergency."

"Yes, I need to report a kidnapping."

Matthew gave as much information as he could as quickly as possible, including the general location in the city and the make, model and color of the car Raven was in. Then he disconnected from the dispatcher and clicked back over to Raven.

"Sonny, please. Slow down. Highway 17 is treacherous."

"Don't worry. There won't be any traffic to worry about getting into a wreck. The only thing down here is the rock quarry. The kids party here on the weekends. But it's pretty well empty through the week."

Highway 17? Where was that? Matthew kept his eye on the road while he leaned across to the glove box for a map of the city and surrounding area. As he sat up, the map tapped the radio, sending a blast of Christian rock into the car.

He fumbled to turn it off, but not soon enough.

"What's that? What's in your pocket?"

"Wait! Sonny!"

"Give it to me. I should have known you were up to something. Hello?" Sonny's voice ranted into the phone.

"Who are you, Sonny? And what are you doing with Raven?"

"What's the matter, Strong? Didn't my baby sister tell you her dirty little secret?"

"What secret are you talking about?"

"Oh, that her mother seduced my father and got herself pregnant. And guess who that baby was?"

"That wasn't Raven's fault, Sonny. She's a good person. I love her."

"I tried to tell you to leave her alone. That she was mine, but you wouldn't listen."

"I know you did, but I misunderstood at the time. How about another chance?"

A short burst of laughter blasted Matt's ear. "You don't catch on too quick. Say goodbye to loverboy."

"I love you, Matt." Raven's sweet voice came through the line just before it went dead.

In a cold sweat, Matthew once again dialed the police.

Chapter Twenty-Three

Raven had never felt such a presence of peace. Even in this danger, she knew God was with her.

The winding road seemed as though it would never end. But that might not be such a bad thing when she was stalling for time. Sonny had tossed her cell phone out the window, so there was no way she'd be able to get Matt back on the phone. He knew where they were headed, though. If only he could get to her in time.

"Sonny, why are you doing this? If what you said to Matt is true, then it seems like you love me and want me to stick around."

"That was before I figured out that you're no better than your mother."

Raven bristled, but bit back a retort. She needed to choose her battle carefully. And the only battle she needed to fight at the moment was the one for her life.

"I'm so sorry if I've hurt you, Sonny. But I never meant to. What did I do to make you hate me so?"

"You exist!" he exploded. "He wouldn't give me the money I needed for the stables. He said that was your inheritance. I mean, it wasn't that much. And I promised to pay it back with interest. But he wouldn't do it. Said he had two kids and he wasn't sacrificing one's inheritance for the other."

Somehow, knowing that warmed Raven. The knowledge that her biological father had at least had some feeling of responsibility for her, if nothing else, showed her he wasn't all bad. "This is about money?"

"Mostly." He cut her a glance. "Sick, isn't it?"

More than he knew. "I don't need or want the money. It's all yours. I'll sign anything you want."

Laughter played in his throat, a hoarse laugh created from years of smoking. "It'll be mine anyway, when you're out of the picture. I didn't know the old man had already put you in his will, or I would have taken care of that first."

"First?" A sickening thud of reality hit Raven's stomach with the velocity of a major-league pitch. "What are you saying?"

"You're the reporter, you figure it out."

"You killed your own dad just to get your hands on some money?"

He shrugged. "I'm not proud of it, Raven, so don't make me out to be a monster."

Was he kidding? Raven watched with incredulity. Horrific truth made all of this so much more real. "Don't you think the police might get a little suspicious if two family members die so close together?"

"No one will be able to connect the two. Dad was mugged in Chicago. I had to teach a class that night."

"What? Did you pay someone?"

"Let's just say someone owed me a favor."

"But why meet me and pretend to want a relationship with me? You could have hired someone to kill me too, and no one would have known any better. Why so much drama?"

Sonny shrugged. "I was going to put a bullet through your heart that night on the road home from Briarwood. You got out at that quick stop and I thought I'd wait and before you got back on the highway, I'd just shoot you then and take off. No one would have seen me. I could have done it, you know. Then I'd have my money, and you would be gone. It would be like finally getting justice for your mother ruining my life."

Raven shuddered, remembering the car that had taken off as she'd come out of the store that night with the bad cup of coffee.

She drew a shaky breath. "What made you change your mind?" Maybe she could play on that and stall for more time. Keep him talking.

"The wind caught your hair and it looked like a sheet lifting up and then down. You were so pretty. Like a doll. And I just wanted to know you. I thought since we were both alone, we could be family for each other. I was your only brother, you were my only sister. I was an idiot."

"But we could have been there for each other, Sonny. We were starting to get to form a relationship, weren't we?"

"Yes, but you wouldn't stop going behind my back to see Strong. I tried everything to make him leave you alone. Even took his little girl. I could have kept her, but I didn't, because a kid shouldn't have to grow up without a parent."

Raven shut her eyes as his words caused all of the pieces to fall together. Somewhere deep inside of him there had to be some decency. Otherwise, there was no telling where Jamie would be today. "Oh, Sonny. You're right. You shouldn't have had to grow up without your mom."

Raven cringed as Sonny's head whipped around. He glared at her. The car wove from one side of the road to the other as his eyes grew wild. "Don't act like you care! It was your mother's fault mine abandoned me. If she hadn't…if she…" Sonny clenched his fists, obviously fighting for control over his raging emotions. He spun off the main highway onto a gravel road. "Anyway, it won't be long now and I'll be able to do what I should have done in the first place. Erase the shame your mother caused mine. Then maybe she'll come back."

He slammed the car to a halt and pulled out his gun. "Get out. Don't bother to run, you'll never find your way out of here." He snagged the keys from the ignition and opened his door.

With another prayer, Raven got out of the car. "Now what?"

"Drink this." He tossed her a bottle of liquor.

"I don't think so."

A roar of rage exploded from him and he grabbed her, pinning her arms behind her back with one massive paw. She gasped as he nearly pulled them from their shoulder sockets. Sonny took the opportunity and tipped the bottle, forcing her to drink. She sputtered and spat, but couldn't keep it all out.

"What are you doing?" she croaked, hoarse from the burning liquid.

"When they find you, they'll think you were loaded with drugs and alcohol and that's why you drove into the quarry—just in case the car doesn't burst into flames."

Raven tried not to focus on the fiery image. Instead she stayed with the plan…stall for time while trying to talk him out of killing her. "Are you kidding me? Sonny, Matt already knows where you are. He heard most of the conversation from the time we left the parking garage. You're not going to get away with this, so why add another murder charge?" Her head was beginning to spin and her words were slurring. She pitched forward, but Sonny caught her. He began walking her around to the driver's side.

"Well, I figure your Matthew is at least twenty minutes behind us. That gives me just enough time to watch this car plunge over the quarry wall, get to my real car, wait for him and then shoot him when he gets here. It's not like anyone's going to hear the gunshot."

Raven felt herself slipping away from the conversation. The liquor he'd forced down her throat must have been drugged, heavily drugged, given how little she'd consumed. She was aware that Sonny had placed her in the driver's side and was belting her in.

"There now, you're all relaxed. You see? I'm not a monster. You'll be completely passed out in just a minute so you won't feel a thing." He reached over her, into the back seat. "And I have a surprise for you. You won't have to die alone."

"Ginger..." Raven mumbled, clutching the stuffed animal to her chest. Ironically, she almost thanked Sonny. But the words refused to take shape on her tongue. As Raven faded, she thought that the next thing she saw would be the face of Jesus.

Matthew sped across the loose gravel, his high beams shining on the blue car just up ahead.

In a moment of horror, he recognized what Sonny was planning to do.

A hoarse cry tore at Matthew's throat as the blue car started to move slowly forward. Matthew knew there wasn't much time. He gunned his own car forward. How close was Raven to the edge of the ravine? "Oh, God. Please help me to get there in time."

A pop sounded in front of him and his windshield glass shattered. A bullet whizzed by his head and he heard the back glass shatter. He ducked and the car swerved. His mind registered that Sonny was shooting at him, but he couldn't be bothered with something like that. Nothing was going to keep him from saving Raven's life.

Matthew made it to the side of the blue car. Then he gunned the accelerator once more. When he cleared the front bumper, he cut the wheels of his sedan and slid to a stop in front of the blue car. The impact forced his car sideways, closer to the quarry. Matthew expelled a relieved breath as it stopped, a few feet from the edge. He had barely enough room to climb out of the driver's side and walk away from the chasm.

He watched Sonny run toward another car.

"Stop and put your hands on your head." The amplified voice called out repeatedly, but Sonny refused to stop. He fired off a round toward the police cars. A volley of gunfire followed. When the air had stopped echoing with shots, Sonny lay flat, staring unseeing at the starry night.

Matthew opened the car door, his heart lodged firmly in his throat at the sight of Raven unconscious in the driver's seat. He reached around her and unbuckled her seatbelt. "Raven, honey. Wake up." He pulled her to him and frowned. She reeked of alcohol.

He looked up at the sound of hard soles on the loose gravel. A young officer squatted down next to him. "Is she all right?"

Matthew snatched up a liquor bottle from the seat next to Raven. "I think he either forced her to drink so much she passed out, or he drugged her."

"Better get her to the hospital to be on the safe side."

The officer looked at the Lexus then back to Matt. "You can ride in the squad car."

Matthew nodded. He lifted Raven into his arms and cradled her against his chest. He'd come too close to losing her for good this time, and he knew he would never let her go again.

The pounding in Raven's head could only be described as the beat of a jackhammer playing inside her brain.

She moaned and slowly opened her eyes. Matt sat in a chair next to her, close enough that he rested his elbows on the bed. She forced her lips into what she hoped was a smile as he captured her gaze.

"Hey, sleepyhead."

"So you finally showed up, huh? I was starting to think I should have called someone else."

Her thick comment elicited just the response she'd hoped for. A low chuckle that always warmed her. "A little feisty for someone who almost went headfirst down a rock pit, wouldn't you say? How'd you think to dial my number anyway? That was pretty smart."

Raven gave him a sleepy smile. "I saw it done once on TV."

"You and TV." He grinned.

Nearly overcome with emotion, Raven felt the rush of tears. "Thank you for saving me."

He leaned in closer, taking her hand. "I'm your knight in shining armor, baby. No way was I going to lose you again." His eyes glistened with unshed tears.

Raven reached out and plunged her fingers through his thick, wavy hair and drew his head downward. He buried his face against the side of her neck. He came up, kissing her cheek, her forehead, her chin, until finally he claimed her lips. Raven sighed against him.

"I feel rotten. What did Sonny give me?"

"We think the date rape drug, only he didn't figure you'd come out of it anyway, so you got too much."

"I ODed?"

"Pretty much. We got you to the hospital just in time."

Raven shuddered. "I need to tell you about Ray."

"Ray?"

"Yeah, he's legit." She gave him the digest version of their encounter at the mission.

"Yeah, I figured all that out."

"Sonny's the man from Adventure Park too."

Matt shook his head. "I was so focused on thinking it was personal, it didn't even occur to me I was being threatened to stay away from you and Jamie wasn't really in danger."

"It's okay. You needed to protect her. It was a natural assumption."

He reached forward and pressed another kiss to her forehead. "I'm going to let your dad and sisters know you're awake."

"Sisters? Is Denni here too?"

"And her husband. The whole family showed up, even Justin and Keri's twins. You are one beloved woman, Raven Mahoney."

"How beloved?" Raven couldn't resist the coquettish question. She didn't want to go another day, another moment without letting Matthew know that he was the one for her. That she'd decided.

He took the bait. "More than any woman has ever been loved since Adam loved Eve."

"Really? And how do you know he loved her? It wasn't like he had any other choices."

"He loved her." Matthew pressed her hand to his lips, and then held her arm against his chest. "She was the woman created for him. He would never have been content with anyone else." His eyes spoke volumes and for once, Raven wasn't afraid to believe the promises they conveyed.

"May I have my ring back?" She whispered the words.

A spark of joy shot to his eyes. "Well, I don't know. That depends."

Raven narrowed her gaze.

"On what?"

"Are you interested in being a political wife?"

Raven squeezed his hand. "Are you going for it again?"

He nodded. "I feel like I have a green light now. I just had to get a few things in my life straightened out before the time was right."

Raven gave a hefty sigh. "It's going to be a real challenge, you know."

He nodded. "I know. But I honestly think I'm supposed to run again."

"Oh, I don't mean your part in all of this. You're going to win by a landslide. I'm the one who has the really hard job. I mean do you realize how much of a challenge it will be to decorate the family floor of the White House."

Matt grinned. "First things first. We have to find our own house for you to decorate."

"So does that mean I get my ring back?"

"It does. When do you want to get married?"

Raven's heart leapt as Matthew leaned closer, his sweet breath warming her face. "The sooner the better," she whispered.

Matthew closed his eyes. "Good answer."

Raven melted into his kiss, relishing her second chance. She refused to think of the wasted years, and simply gave thanks to God that He was restoring back to her everything she'd almost lost. Today was a fresh new day. Tomorrow was bright. And whatever the future held for them, she knew one thing, the greatest joy would be loving Matthew for the rest of her life.

Epilogue

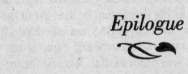

On Thanksgiving Day, not a sound could be heard in the Mahoney Cabin as Mac Mahoney reached out and took hold of his bride's hand. The Southern belle glowed with a beauty that went beyond the layers of makeup caking her face.

Raven, Denni and Keri stood next to her, arm-in-arm as they listened to Mac finally reciting his vows.

Raven imagined her mother's beautiful pale face, so like Keri's. She had raised them, had loved them and had loved Mac until her dying day. But Raven knew her mother would never want Mac to go through his twilight years all alone...not if he could love again. And he did. The sparkle in his eyes as he slipped the ring on Ruth's finger said it all.

Raven glanced out at the small gathering of family and friends, who had all taken time out of their Thanksgiving Day to share in the Mahoney family's joy. The reception would be a Thanksgiving feast.

They all had so much to be thankful for this year. Keri's Justin and her two ten-year-old boys, Josh and Billy, sat in the front row. Contentment shone in all three faces. It was difficult to believe that only two years earlier, Justin had been fighting to prove he hadn't killed his unfaithful wife.

Denni's handsome cop, Reece, winked at his wife. Raven couldn't stop a smile from forming on her lips. Married less than a year and Denni was already going to have a baby. Her stomach already showed signs of roundedness. It was fitting that Denni be the first of the three girls to bear her own child. She had inherited all of Mom's ability to nurture and love and care for others. Mahoney House was proof of that. A home for former foster-care girls, it provided a safe place as the young women made the transition from wards of the state to adulthood.

With a sigh, Raven turned her gaze to her own little family. Matthew stared back at her, no doubt remembering, as she was, their own wedding ceremony at the Strong mansion two weeks after her ordeal with Sonny. Much to Raven's delight, Aunt Meredith had attended.

Next to Raven, Jamie squirmed, no doubt ready to be free of the pink flower-girl dress she lamented over. She'd proclaimed herself too old to be a flower girl and no way would she wear a dress. But some fast talking, bribery and the promise that she could lose the dress as soon as the ceremony ended had finally convinced the little beauty to acquiesce.

A round of applause rang in the air as Mac and Ruth were pronounced man and wife. Mac Mahoney kissed his bride tenderly.

"Okay, y'all," Ruth drawled. "Time for pictures. I want the whole family up here, pronto, while these kids are still looking fancy."

Ten minutes of chaos ensued. Raven was jostled and poked and shoved until finally she stood with Matthew behind her, his arms encircling her waist. "Hey, beautiful," he whispered in her ear.

Raven released a contented sigh as the camera flashed. Matthew nuzzled her neck and she turned in his arms and accepted his kiss.

"Hey, now. You're making us look bad!" Justin protested before snatching his own wife for a sweet kiss.

"I guess weddings just bring out the romance in some guys," Reece said. "I'm a romantic all the time."

"Yes you are, my darling." Denni raised her face to his.

Laughter and catcalls lifted into the air as the three Mahoney sisters rested in their husbands' arms.

Raven's heart sang as she looked around at her wonderful family. The laughter and love seemed to foreshadow the years that lay ahead. Her children and those of her sisters would grow up together knowing they were safe, secure and loved.

She felt a warm hand on her shoulder and she smiled, recognizing the gentle touch of her father. She turned and sank into a tight embrace. Words weren't necessary. This man was her father. She held him tightly, conveying all the love she felt for him and accepting his love for her.

With a kiss on her forehead, he let her go. Matthew slipped his arm about her shoulders and she leaned her head against his shoulder. "Thank you for waiting for me, Matthew."

"Thank you for not making me wait any longer."

His eyes sparkled with love. He was about to move in for another kiss when Jamie's disgusted voice broke through the moment.

"Oh, brother. All this kissy-kissy stuff is making me sick. I probably won't be able to eat any turkey."

Once again, laughter exploded in the room. Raven

gave her new daughter a quick squeeze. "Just wait until your time comes, sport. Your heart will make the choice for you. You'll never be happy until you give in."

Raven looked deeply into Matthew's eyes as she spoke. Her heart overflowed with happiness.

* * * * *

Dear Reader,

Thank you for joining me for the third and final book in The Mahoney Sisters series. I never fail to marvel at the love of adoptive parents for their children. Chosen children. Children, who were born to one family, but planted firmly in another. Legally, they are given the same right to the surname and anything their parents have just as though they shared a bloodline.

This is exactly what Jesus does for us. His blood is like an adoption certificate, legally binding us into the family God. We were not God's original family, but He chose us to become His children. What an awesome gift. We are heirs of salvation. Joint heirs with Jesus.

This is what Raven had to come to understand. That she was part of the Mahoney family just as surely as if she'd been born into Mac Mahoney's bloodline. He took her as his daughter, raised her as his own, loved her as his own and gave her his name. She *was* his daughter. All she had to do was come to an understanding of how much Mac loved her. How often do we doubt that God really loves us, that He really wants good things for us? I pray that as you read this book, the "father" love of God spoke to your heart in a special way.

God bless you as you live, move and have your being in Him.

Tracey V. Bateman

Take 2 inspirational love stories FREE!

PLUS get a FREE surprise gift!

Mail to Steeple Hill Reader Service™

In U.S.
3010 Walden Ave.
P.O. Box 1867
Buffalo, NY 14240-1867

In Canada
P.O. Box 609
Fort Erie, Ontario
L2A 5X3

YES! Please send me 2 free Love Inspired® novels and my free surprise gift. After receiving them, if I don't wish to receive anymore, I can return the shipping statement marked cancel. If I don't cancel, I will receive 4 brand-new novels every month, before they're available in stores! Bill me at the low price of $4.24 each in the U.S. and $4.74 each in Canada, plus 25¢ shipping and handling and applicable sales tax, if any*. That's the complete price and a savings of over 10% off the cover prices—quite a bargain! I understand that accepting the books and gift places me under no obligation ever to buy any books. I can always return a shipment and cancel at any time. Even if I never buy another book from Steeple Hill, the 2 free books and the surprise gift are mine to keep forever.

113 IDN DZ9M
313 IDN DZ9N

Name	(PLEASE PRINT)	
Address	Apt. No.	
City	State/Prov.	Zip/Postal Code

Not valid to current Love Inspired® subscribers.

Want to try two free books from another series?
Call 1-800-873-8635 or visit www.morefreebooks.com.

* Terms and prices are subject to change without notice. Sales tax applicable in New York. Canadian residents will be charged applicable provincial taxes and GST. All orders subject to approval. Offer limited to one per household.

® are registered trademarks owned and used by the trademark owner and or its licensee.

INTLI04R

©2004 Steeple Hill

Love Inspired
SUSPENSE

TITLES AVAILABLE NEXT MONTH

Don't miss these two stories in November

SHADOW BONES by Colleen Rhoads
Great Lakes Legends

Skye Blackbird was convinced she'd find diamonds in her family's mine. Paleontologist Jake Baxter felt the same about fossils. When the site was sabotaged, Jake didn't know who to blame. Someone didn't want the earth disturbed, but it also seemed that someone might not want him or Skye alive...

HER BROTHER'S KEEPER by Valerie Hansen

Becky Tate finds the new preacher charming. But though he's ordained, Logan Malloy has never preached before! He's undercover, investigating whether Becky was kidnapped as an infant. He has to find the truth without ruining the only family Becky knows—and hurting the woman he's come to love....